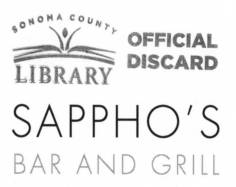

SONOMA COUNTY
LIBRARY **OFFICIAL DISCARD**

SAPPHO'S
BAR AND GRILL

Bonnie J. Morris

Bywater
BOOKS

Ann Arbor
2017

Bywater Books

Print ISBN: 978-1-61294-097-7

Bywater Books First Edition: June 2017

Printed in the United States of America on acid-free paper.

Quote on page 143: Barbara Mayer Wertheimer. *We Were There: The Story of Working Women in America*. NY: Pantheon, 1977, p. 21.

E-Book ISBN: 978-1-61294-098-4

Cover designer: Ann McMan, TreeHouse Studio

Bywater Books
PO Box 3671
Ann Arbor MI 48106-3671
www.bywaterbooks.com

This novel is a work of fiction.

for all my friends and loved ones at Herizon,
the original Sappho's Bar;

for Liz Harter and Jane Collins,

and for two of our best amazon history travelers,
Lillian Faderman and Alison Bechdel.

Table of Contents

Chapter One
Valentine's Day

"Professor Stern. Will this be on the midterm exam?"

The question came from a young woman Hannah knew hadn't been to class for the practice test on great women in history: a psych major who always sent e-mails at 1:00 a.m. the night before papers were due, complaining that deadlines were linear and oppressive. Laptops temporarily forgotten, the other 106 first-year women's history students looked up at their professor like so many blinking barn owls, fingers hovering in suspense. If it wasn't on the midterm, they wouldn't write it down.

Remember, you can watch an old movie tonight, Hannah reminded herself as she outlined, for the fourth time, exactly which text chapters and which famous women the class should review. *You can stop by the bar for one drink with Isabel first. Then you can pick up some ice cream or gingerbread. You have a big, unopened jar of Italian lemon honey that Gail left behind.* But this passing thought hurt more than it soothed. Leftover honey from her last honey would have the taste of a rebuke, not a reward.

She folded papers into her leather briefcase as a lingering group of students clustered around her. "Will you grade on a curve? Will attendance count for our final grade? I mean, I come to class even when I'm sick. Like, I actually have mono right now, but I'm here, okay?" In her peripheral vision, Hannah could see the furious face of the exchange student who had publicly charged her with "reinforcing gender binaries"—the ultimate crime. Whatever happened to the good old days when women's studies students had crushes on tired dyke professors? These days, most students just wanted an easy A. Others seemed to take sadistic pleasure in correcting her, mid-lecture, with facts gleaned from laptop Wikipedia pages: material they preferred to the reading she carefully planned, assigned, and distributed hot from the ancient photocopier in Irwin Hall.

She grabbed her green suede jacket and headed for the faculty parking lot and the safe sanctuary of her twenty-year-old Honda Civic, a limping animal held together with outdated feminist bumper stickers. Once inside, she sank behind the wheel, ripped off her bra (a ritual indicating the teaching day had officially ended), and cranked up a CD by the cover band called Lez Zeppelin. Strains of "Kashmir" thudded.

Burned out didn't come close to describing her state of mind.

The initials were right, though; take your pick. Boiling Over. Bailing Out. Body Odor. Breaking Off—yes, she was brittle. Time to go see Isabel, to unwind at the coolest bar in the world—and, driving over to the familiar watering hole across town, Hannah freely indulged in shouting colorful insults at every car driver and bike messenger (all men) who got in her way. Toadstool! Slime spore! Lotus blossom! Milkpod! Earth furrow! Moletail! She loved the organic garden-variety slurs that Isabel began using in lieu of fouler language, back when they were in graduate school together and had the opportunity to interview several very old nuns. (At their first appointment in the convent library archive, Hannah had accidentally dropped a priceless medieval Bible onto her big toe and shrieked, "God damn it to fucking *shit*, that hurt" in resounding alto. She was not invited back.)

All that seemed a lifetime ago when both of them were so young, hopeful. Isabel had burned out of the academic track first—rather mysteriously resigning from her graduate research assistantship and leaving their Ph.D. program in women's history

2

to go work in a tough lesbian bar, waiting out the original owners until they retired to Florida, and then buying the bar herself with a loan from the only rich friend they knew. Iz renamed it Sappho's Bar and Grill, completely repaneling the interior and stocking the shelves with souvenir bottles from the world's best lesbian clubs. The bottles now gleamed amid rare antiquarian books with lesbian storylines, so that on any given night one could read hot erotica from eighteenth-century France while swirling a bit of cognac pinched from the Paris Katmandu Club or chicory coffee-infused crème de cacao from Charlene's New Orleans bar. And there amid the history of all women before them who had dared to love one another, Isabel seemed very much at peace, serving delicious mixed drinks found nowhere else and dispensing wisdom and first-edition books to a loyal clientele. The bar had a smoking patio (for women who loved brandy and cigars) and discreet spaces for romantic interludes.

You didn't have to love books, gay history, or herbal mixology to find a home at Sappho's. The regulars included cool women of every race and class from the four surrounding towns. But Isabel had built something there, a radical hospitality, a place that professors and policewomen, artists, and softball coaches all returned to for comfort in times of sorrow or celebration. Hannah was headed to Sappho's now, hoping a drink with her old friend (they had not been lovers, despite all the flirtatious energy Hannah employed back in the day) would take the edge off her sadly familiar mood: the stymied, dinosauric exhaustion of an aging and underpaid women's studies professor.

Anything was better than heading home. Her datebook was full, but not, alas, with dates. The kitchen cupboards were empty, other than the leftover souvenir food: jams and teas and coffees she and Gail had picked up in Wales, Brazil, and Newfoundland. Almost two years since Gail walked out—and now, several additional inches around the waistline into her forties, was Hannah hungry for a curvy woman or a square meal? Or the flat plane of a café table, the familiar dining nook at Sappho's? Would Hannah ever lean across that table again to tell Gail bits of university

3

gossip, to regale her with scandals just to see her eyes crinkle with laughter?

Unlikely. Over and done. Gail had walked out and there was nothing to do but eat the jar of honey and remember the good times. Hannah took a left turn on two wheels, glancing up at the enormous radio tower, which dominated the tier of hills on the south side of the university town. Forever and ever, that radio tower signal would make her think of her failed relationship, the days and nights she lay in bed in a stupor of disbelief that it was over, watching the red light blink atop the distant tower jutting up from the hillside. Funny how girders of steel silhouetted against a dusky sky could instantly make Hannah think of (and miss) a warm, long-legged human being. She tried to opt out of the parade of associations in her mind, scrambling around for a memory that had nothing to do with Gai. There had been other women in her life, many before Gail. But none since.

On top of everything else, Hannah remembered, her students' winter midterms fell on the anniversary of her father's death this year. Yes, that date was coming up again. It seemed that nothing in a professor's schedule made room for everyday acts of utter devastation: grief, loss, being dumped. When her father died, four Februaries ago, Hannah's entire apartment was in disarray and covered with smelly drop cloths, as the building management had selected that very month to rewire everyone's walls. She had wept and made calls and sent cards to relatives while callous electricians buzzed in and out unannounced, flinging dust and grit and duct tape in their wake, a thin layer of dirt caulking her mourning. On the first anniversary of her father's passing she meant to do something thoughtful and serious, a private ritual at the ocean, and instead had that inconvenient skin rash, as if grief were an allergic reaction or an uninvited flea circus in her flesh. Then came year three without her dad: the year when Gail walked out. And this year, her computer had crashed. Everything she'd ever written, including the one poem she'd finally started for her father, now lay scattered on the floor of her university office in pieces: flash drives, disks, and cables. All she wanted was *one week* for a sense of love and mourning, for ritual apartness—nothing itching, nothing stalled or broken.

Well, fuck that—it wasn't going to happen. She was never going to get that parentheses of focus and feeling in some quiet time tunnel, not in her hectic, pressured life. *Fine.* She would carry on with a rock for a heart and a thumb drive for a mind, a living axe and adze, an Amazon labrys chopping toward clarity through the woods of women's history, severed branches and twigs of feminist rage hacked off in trails behind her like some perverse Camp Fire Girl outing. She would carry unfulfilled desire on her back like a camel's hump of water, sipping incrementally as she plodded over hills. Her lovers would be imaginary, the great heroines of the past, the figures in her women's history lectures; yes, they would do for now. Yet if her own personal history was turning out to be so painful, how could she believe she was still equipped to translate for 200 freshmen the enormous mammarian battles of women's past?

Bullshit, thought Hannah, pulling into the rear parking lot at the bar and switching off her ignition. She was safe, warm, dry; she really had little to complain about. No one was threatening to set her poetry on fire or to torture her at the stake; she was neither enslaved to an abusive master nor bound by laws that named her infidel, criminal pervert, witch. Her mind flicked over the roster of women's names from the not-yet-xeroxed midterm. She just wished she could talk to the women she daily talked *about,* and get some hearty personal advice on how they had survived *their* life trials—trials so much scarier than anything Hannah ever faced in the contained fluorescent world of a well-lit lecture hall. At most, her daily torture was a splinter from that podium in Building B. She marveled at such bravery from the past; it was what had led her, after a youth of suburban middle-class comforts, to major in what her radical feminist classmates called *herstory.*

For one minute she sat in the warm car, now silent with the wailing Lez music turned off, her breath just beginning to make faint steam as the outer February air pushed in. She had arrived.

Yes, Hannah had a place to go—the local bar—and a tribe she belonged to in her own time: the lesbian community, gaining civil rights strengths every day. She wasn't isolated socially or politically. Love: well, it might come again. Or not. But somehow, as a teacher, she felt isolated now, with still so much to pass along to students clearly tired of her zeal. Ah, why couldn't Sappho herself just mystically show up as a substitute teacher in a nice toga and sandals, taking over the next day's lecture on ancient Lesbos, so that Hannah could lie down and talk to her father's ghost? And if Hannah's life mission had always been getting the dead to speak across time through historical interpretation, could she get her father to intercede in the great beyond and shift some lesbian ghosts to bank her fires? Did he have a direct line to Sappho that Hannah herself lacked, being alive and cranky and itchy? And alone?

She heaved herself out, locked the ungraded papers in her car, and went in.

The bar was just beginning to fill up: two young Latina women on a butch-femme date; four middle school cafeteria lunch ladies playing eight-ball at the pool table; a labor lawyer who waved at Hannah and then returned to her everlasting argument with the local orchestra conductor. The noise, laughter, and neat click of pool balls filled Hannah with comfort and familiarity. She could close her eyes and know where she was by sound and scent, the voices, the dried herbs and flowers braided around the posts holding up the carved bar awning, and of course Letty in the corner by the heater, pausing mid-cackle to blow her enormous nose, a terrifying bass note blast with the sustained intensity of an island foghorn. Old Letty, the bar's venerable elder Amazon, was one of just two regulars from the bar's earliest years, and the only one to protest certain changes under Isabel's management: specifically, the introduction of live plants. Isabel's herbal-infused drinks and horticultural bar décor turned out to be an itchy problem for Letty, who suffered from hay fever all year long. But, ever the old-school good sport, she had grudgingly shown up for Grand Reopening night and sneezed like hellfire for two hours, just to taste the rare juniper in the gin. "Well, I'll say it's different, all right. It's got a taste like—*Achoo.* Whatevah," she'd hawed and hemmed with afflicted resignation, glass raised high in tribute to Isabel's fern-topped concoctions. "You sure gotta love the—*h'choo!* this fancy fungus. Kinda gives ya an extra high, don't it? It's just I'm allergic to the whatsit she puts in her booze. But yeah, pour me another, why not? Boy, I'm feeling no pain." The very next night, Isabel mixed a hot buttered gin just for Letty, and shifted one particular flowering plant from the bar to the terrarium underneath the pool table. And for the first time in her long life Letty stopped sneezing and started winning at pool.

Now as Hannah waved to Letty, other voices called out to her: "Yo, doc!" "Stern! Get a brew and come over here; we need you for pinochle!" "Hey, professor—where's Ginger and Mary Ann?" Nobody ever called her Hannah. Absurdly, the theme song from "Cheers" ran through her mind: *Sometimes you want to go where everybody knows your name . . .*

But friendly razzing was just a part of Sappho's. It had bewildered her when she first arrived in upstate New York, all the teasing and good-natured knocks to pride, so different from her northern California upbringing. When she remained clumsily unsure how to distinguish genuine insult from genuine flirtation, Zak the Animal took pity on her and gave her a lesson—Betty Zakhour, Isabel's first bouncer, a huge behemoth of a rugby player with an equally big heart. "Look, doc," growled Zak, "these women? They like you. They're just busting your chops, just whaling on you." "Thank you," Hannah had replied politely, wondering: *Busting? Whaling? What does it all mean?* How green she was. Now, years later, she knew enough to reply to any tossed barb with timed insouciance: "Yeah, right. Don't hurt yourself."

This was home away from home now. She scraped a bar stool under herself and looked down the freshly buffed counter to find her beloved friend, the barkeep, owner, and host.

"Hi, Iz. What it is."

"What it *was.*"

"Make me a mocktail that tells the truth."

"Do you want absinthe or do you want vermouth?"

They had kept up their old comedy routine since they were twenty-five, for almost two full decades now. Hannah and Isabel had taken the same women's history courses in grad school, could cite the same books, reflect back on the same crusty eccentric beloved professors, dish on old classmates who had fled feminist scholarship for law school or software startups or partnered bliss. But for all their shared history, Isabel had a history of her own—a backstory nobody knew and which she only revealed in stray, pearl-like asides. Her parents weren't alive any more, but she spoke of them reverently. They were—German? Austrian? French? Definitely Catholic. Isabel had briefly been a nun, before grad school—or, depending on the story, a very young novice. Then she'd abandoned the convent or, in another rumor, had been expelled, caught "experimenting" with a sister novice and sent packing. She still maintained all the austerity of her convent years in her loft studio apartment, sleeping alone under a massive portrait of Joan of Arc, rising at 5:00 a.m. to brew her own beer, boil flavored syrups and mixes for cocktails, and then prepare all the food sold at the bar. Everyone loved and wanted her, hearts and yonis alike thudding when she greeted customers. She was famous for gently saying no to every proposition while loving everyone. As far as Hannah knew, in their twenty-year friendship Isabel had never been partnered, yet who knew what went on in the Nook of the bar?

Isabel, eyes sometimes gray, more often green, warm and inquiring, now poured Hannah a shot of Bailey's on ice, then tapped the rim with her own antique goblet water glass in a quick toast, another old ritual. "*Salud et l'chaim.* Thinking about your father this week?"

Hannah knew then that she looked as sad as she felt. "No, thinking about Gail. Thinking about students who hate women's history and who plagiarize facts on the founding of Rome from Italian restaurant menus. Thinking about the 106 papers I have to grade before the Valentine's Day party here. Which I will once

8

again attend ALONE, barring Cupid's arrow in my ass between now and Friday."

"Ah. Same old, then."

"Yeah."

They sipped in silence, and Hannah lowered her eyes to Isabel's hands, the flower rings she wore. Hands that had, regrettably, never explored Hannah's breasts and thighs, despite her idiotic pleading during their one European vacation together back in 1986: *Please, Iz, just once before I die. And Iz, what if I die tomorrow?*

Isabel moved away to ring up a beer for another bar patron who had entered, then returned to assess Hannah's brooding. "Hey, you. I know you like to complain, and often with good reason; but at heart you like the pressure and you love teaching. You always did—more than I knew I would. Don't you still?"

"Yeah. But what do I do with all these student papers that begin, 'There were no lesbians before Ellen DeGeneres came out'? They don't see the history I teach them."

"Do *you* see the history you teach them?"

This was a good question. Damn Isabel. Had Hannah lost her sense of the women she lectured on? "The great women of history." No matter how she rearranged her ever-changing syllabus, shifted and split its sections like paramecia, adding women from this region and that era, struggled to balance Global North with Global South, women of color with pre-Christian Europe's witches, inventors and healers, servants and slaves, athletes and queens, concubines and conservatives, innkeepers and film stars, some group was bound to be left out and she would always feel she'd failed in representing them. Where had her love of women's history begun? As a child when she heard Shirley Chisholm speak? No. Earlier. The babysitter who read her the book about female pirates. No, she had loved the babysitter. The babysitter and the pirate were one. She was feeling the drink, though the drink was a very small one. Isabel always made her little fancy drinks with something extra in them that acted on Hannah like truth serum; here it was, happening again. She was relaxed, her worries and the stress of the empty apartment at home forgotten, but the unanswered question swirling around her like a drop of paint in a water glass. Who did she see? When she stood in front of the women's history classroom, who guided her?

In truth, her deepest muse was probably Sappho, if not another lesbian from the ancient past. The sense of obligation to get her own people into the record had been an urgent mandate since graduate school. For all their excellent education, Hannah and Isabel had just missed the coming wave of LGBT studies, had been too early, then too late, and the frosty paperwork demanded of anyone daring to attempt a *lesbian dissertation* so irked Isabel that she dropped out to serve the women's community directly. "You write about us; I'll nourish us," had been her apology to Hannah. The homophobic pushback they encountered even in a women's history graduate program had only made Hannah dig in further. She was the first in their cohort to grab her credentials and start teaching, young, enraged, her sweater always buttoned wrong, one earring falling out, but love of scholarship blasting from her fingers as she retyped lecture notes for her assigned classes. She felt motivated—indeed, *haunted*—by Sappho's poetic fragment: "You may forget but/Let me tell you/this: someone in/some future time/will think of us." Nearly every day, she stood in front of her students and wrote these lines on the blackboard in tough-looking purple chalk. Never mind the groans and the whispers: "Oh, no, not Sappho again." "She's obsessed!"

The bar was a place to unwind with a few other professors and old friends. Gail had not really liked it; it was part of the reason they broke up, Hannah reflected now. The endless tug between The Community and The Relationship, between loving women and loving one woman. Hating conflict, Hannah remained passive, unhappily turning over their problems in her mind. Gail took action, demanding "Choose!" and then walking out.

Hannah stood up. No wallowing in regret and failure: There were papers to grade. This was supposed to be a one-drink, quick-visit night. She felt woozy, though, and now Isabel pointed out that she had not eaten anything, had driven from work after a long teaching day, and then lit into a drink on an empty stomach. "Come and eat," said Isabel. "I'm firing up the grill for a bunch of other women coming in later. They ordered roast vegetables with herbs. I set aside some potatoes and beets for you. And sour cream, of course." She beckoned to what they called The Nook, a side room with a rustic table for intimate dinners or romantic discussions by candlelight. Lured by the promise of Jewish comfort food, grateful that Isabel always knew what she wanted and needed, Hannah stumbled around the back of the bar and sat down at the hidden wooden table.

But someone was already there. It looked like—

It was Sappho.

No. It wasn't. How ridiculous. Hannah blinked. It was some woman in a Sappho outfit. Now she recognized Jeri, one of their university friends from the art department, sprawled out in a toga and garland. "Surprise!" she shouted. "How do you like this costume? Isabel told me to bring it over for you. It's for the Valentine's Day party! If you want it, you can borrow it."

"Jesus, Jeri," Hannah said faintly. "Where did you get something like that?"

"Yeah, looks real, huh? I mean authentic. Got it on eBay, kiddo! I was one of the Muses at the art department graduation party last May, remember? Aren't you always reminding us that Plato called Sappho the Tenth Muse? So we thought you could wear this next weekend." Jeri was peeling off the toga and sandals, revealing her more familiar evening yoga clothing. "Ahhh . . . that's better. You do feel the weight of women's history in this rig!"

"Hannah feels the weight of it all the time, even in her pajamas," Isabel called over her shoulder.

"Fuck you," Hannah returned, quickly adding "I mean, *desist, ye mocking toadstool,*" and they laughed. "Okay. You're right. Actually, I do like it. I'll wear it to the party. After all, I'm between girlfriends, and my longest love really is women's history. Let's drink to that. *Women's history will be my date this year!*"

And Isabel, smiling to herself in the recess behind the bar, added: *So mote it be.* But nobody heard her.

When Hannah showed up to the dance in her Sapphic toga, Jeri, Megan, Sylvia, Dog, and Yvette let out shrieks and whistles of appreciation. "Girl, you look *ancient!*" Dog called out.

"Thanks," Hannah replied. "That's great. That's sure to attract younger women."

"She means you look like a real lesbo, from Lesbos," Megan assured.

Should I have worn underwear? Hannah wondered.

She took the drink that Isabel handed her (something pink, with gold-flecked red hearts in the beveled goblet glass, in honor of the holiday) and sipped sedately, mindful of not spilling on her borrowed finery. Couples entered the bar, laughing, guffawing as dykes do, hand-slapping and hugging, peeling off winter leather jackets and bulky down coats to reveal outfits clearly representing their alter egos and avatars: cowgirl, stripper, auto mechanic (but that was Sherry's actual job—no fair, thought Hannah); Mafia don, Rosie the Riveter, the pope, Marilyn Monroe, Snow White. Old Letty arrived well-guarded against the occasion's romantic flower arrangements, costumed in a skin-diving mask and snorkel, with her elegant partner, Glo, dressed as a giant clam (a pearl clenched in her false teeth.) The disco ball lit up in crimson-washed sparkles as Isabel's eclectic music list for the evening drew new arrivals to the wooden dance floor platform: Etta James, "In the Basement"; Holly Near, "Bony Jaw Baby"; Lorraine Segato, "Mama Quilla"; Sheila E, "The Glamorous Life." Rosie the Riveter and Snow White were soon making out on what they all called the pit furniture, low sofas always at the ready for impulsive necking (and impossible to get out of quickly, as Hannah had discovered once when she was wrapped in a new girlfriend and the woman's ex stormed in.) The pope was on top of and then rapidly underneath Marilyn Monroe. The cowgirl and Xena Warrior Princess were dancing barefoot despite the snow outside the bar, confetti churning beneath their feet. Splashes of Isabel's mystic cocktails reddened dancers' cheeks—both faces and exposed rear ends in naughty-cut chaps. The disco ball turned, turned. And Hannah felt the approaching twin harbingers of a night out at Sappho's Bar and Grill: a surreal wash of dizziness, paired with the sad knowledge she was once again alone among the coupled.

In the corner was a middle-aged dyke who looked very familiar in a horrible sort of way. Hannah squinted. It must be someone who showed up fairly often. She seemed at home in the bar. Shoes like Hannah's, probably ordered from the same hip-twelve-years-ago catalog. She wore a jacket like Hannah's, too. *Wait a minute. God damn it.* A hot plume of embarrassment curled up Hannah's collarbone. One of their busting, whaling prankster pals had actually come to the Valentine's dance *costumed as Hannah!*

The woman smiled. "Yes. I am you. No?"

Oh, how embarrassing. *How fucking embarrassing.* The woman had to be one of the university's graduate exchange students—or, more likely, one of the visiting faculty scholars Hannah had not met yet. She struggled to be polite. After all, any new academic colleague willing to come to the Valentine's dance in a lesbian bar was worth knowing. Hard to place the accent: Croatian? Portuguese? Damn. Who had dressed her up like Hannah? It had to be impish Isabel. Only she would have in her possession an entire outfit's worth of forgotten, unstylish garments Hannah had left behind at the bar over the past ten years. Sighing, she approached her doppelganger.

"I must look *hideous,* daily, if that's typical of the ensembles I throw together. Please trust me, I have nicer clothes at home. I have things that match; I do. Uh . . . like a black dress. Yeah. I don't know why I dress so drab. I teach so much I never have time to go shopping . . ."

The woman was laughing, and her laugh was beautiful. Bewitching, in fact. "But one's own clothes look loveliest on oneself. So your own clothes may look lovely on you. Perhaps we switch now? I will disrobe and give you back."

"Well, but—whoa, no need to get naked, now," Hannah sputtered, as the woman threw off her dowdy outfit, the sudden pile of fleece puddling on the scarred floor between them. "Wait a minute. Wow. You look great, but, hey, slow down. Look, I'm already dressed up. For once, I dressed up! Let me explain, and you can just put your clothes back on. I mean, my clothes. I can't swap outfits right now; I'm in a special costume too. You see, I'm supposed to be—"

"Sappho," said the beautiful and now naked Greek woman, holding out her hand in introduction. "At last we meet." She moved away from the cushioned club chair and toward Hannah, adding, "Yes, soon, you can dress me. As myself. But not yet." She took Hannah in her arms. "Not yet, my darling one."

And then the disco lights faded. They were somewhere else. What had been the dance music of "We Are Family" was now the strum of a lyre. And the flavor in her mouth was not Isabel's bar cocktail but an astringent *retsina*, a taste that seemed to seep from the wise, soft lips on her own open mouth. Hannah felt a Mediterranean wind and the hot light pouring over pines and olive trees, carrying a scent of olive wood and olive oil and grape vines and hyacinths. Everything was rustling, branches, togas, vines—and then the bits of confetti kicked up from the dance floor of the bar turned into a sudden shower of page fragments. Bits and bits of shredded, burnt pages were falling from the air, blown around Sappho's hair and landing on her shoulders. Hannah, dizzy from the intense sensation of time shift, her breath buried under Sappho's timeless kiss, reached down to hold the woman's creased brown hands, rough from endless hours of weaving, but there was no skin to hold onto—only fragments of burnt paper. Sappho's hands were poems.

"I know they burned your writing," Hannah said, not knowing what else to say or how long the moment might last. "I can't think of anything more frightening, or more violent. To be erased by your inheritors, who should be teaching you."

"But you teach me every day," said Sappho. "Don't you? I am told you write my poems on your board almost every day. And every night they wash it off, erase me, and every day you write it out again. You are like a myth from my own time. Rolling the rock uphill, over and over, though it may roll back against you. I know these ways. Why are you bringing me back to life every day in that room?"

"I have to," Hannah fumbled to explain, aware of Sappho's fingers on her body, warm fingers that were no longer paper poems. "I made a sort of commitment, when I—when I read you. You said someday someone would think of you. And I've made sure that others think of you."

"So," the lyric poet smiled. "Of course I come to you tonight. It is the night of couples, is it not? And you are so convinced you are alone." She gestured, and more fragments flew upward from her palms. "How do you like my island?"

This can't be happening, thought Hannah, her tongue in Sappho's mouth. But when she reopened her eyes she saw them, three spare and sullen priests approaching through the grove, all holding torches. "Run!" hissed Sappho. "That way. To the cave. Run and write me! Write me on the board!" Then Hannah was in a rough cool hollow of cliff wall, her back to the damp stone and her heart pounding. A young girl looked up, startled, interrupted in the act of chalking lyrics on the wall. "Shhhh," cautioned Sappho's daughter Cleis. "Wait."

Seconds or centuries later Hannah was watching balls of burning parchment roll down the walls of Isabel's bar. No—*Sappho's Bar.* Isabel had bought the place and registered it as Sappho's Bar and Grill. Once upon a time, though, in that ancient world, Sappho's poetry had been both barred and grilled, grilled for public delight by self-righteous new believers who loathed her for her lyric love of women.

"I love women, too," Hannah told the air, which danced with paper, and it was not burning parchment after all. Just bright crepe paper Isabel had strung, loosed and torn by laughing couples kissing, dancing, eating cake. Sappho was gone, leaving Hannah's bad clothes in a heap on the floor. But when Hannah looked in the mirror she had a love bite on her neck, just at the scoop of her Sapphic toga. It was the shape of a Greek letter: a lambda, the curving L of Lesvos. It lasted for five days.

That was the first time; or what Hannah came to think of as the first *incident*. Other *incidents* followed, as regular or irregular as her own unpredictable menstrual period in appearance. And after a while it became normal. She would go to the bar after a particularly gruesome class, a lecture where she gave her all, and for some reason it just sat there, ignored and avoided by the students—and she'd feel the sting that women's history now was so unvalued. Isabel would concoct some delicacy, some drink with just a hint of wonder, and strange things would happen. It seemed one night, for instance, that she, Hannah, was sitting at the bar gazing into her own reflection in the mirror behind the bar, observing how she was growing old and gaining strands of gray, and suddenly on either side of her were women in that mirror. Glorious women, figures from the past: queens from her own lectures, priestesses, or radical suffragists. One night she was certain she saw Joan of Arc to her left, their shoulders almost touching, and when she turned there was no one of course; all that remained was a faint scent of burning flesh. A scent Hannah would not forget.

But they never talked about it. They never talked about where Isabel went when she disappeared for an hour at her own bar, or what the herbs were that made the drinks change colors in your mouth. A game had been set in motion on that night when Hannah came in and asked for truths to quench her sense of burnout. It was easy to play along with Isabel and float. It was the way they once handled the attraction they had never acted on, feeling everything, saying nothing, Isabel in charge, Hannah completely clueless and out of control.

Chapter Two

The Passover Seder

Can it be
I am the only Jew residing in Danville, Kentucky,
looking for matzoh in the Safeway and the A & P?
Maxine Kumin, 1972

"Hey, Al! *AL!* Do we have a price on this box of the giant-size Saltines?" the checkout clerk bellowed, impatiently waving Hannah's box of matzah in the air until each delicate sheet inside cracked, split, and crumbled. Hannah felt her face burn as everyone in the grocery store turned and stared. Once again, she was going to be outed as the Jew at Safeway, forced to explain the culinary conditions of her foremothers' flight from Egypt. Hannah heard the customer behind her sigh and mutter; *her* selection of lurid-pink marshmallow Easter peeps was recognizable, socially approved.

The student manager hurried over to inspect and identify the mysterious groceries that were holding up the line on a busy Thursday night. On the conveyer belt, next to the "giant Saltines," were Hannah's neatly bagged selections of parsley, horseradish, apples, walnuts and Manischewitz wine. Aha!

Al happened to be one of Hannah's old students. Now he burst

17

out laughing and lifted Hannah's box of matzah for all to see. "'This is the bread of affliction that my foremothers took with them out of Egypt,'" he quoted to the store of gaping customers.

"Amen," agreed Hannah, startled and grateful.

"Matzah is the most important part of the menu for a Passover Seder," Al told the checkout clerk. "These aren't just big crackers. It's the special unleavened bread for the Passover holiday week," and he handed the box back to Hannah, reciting: "'In every generation, it is the duty of each woman to consider herself as if she had come forth from Egypt.' Happy holidays, Dr. Stern."

She had never felt so affirmed, so loved, standing there in her old snow pants at Safeway, her eyes filling with tears, her former student ringing up the right price for their heritage in a box.

By Saturday night Hannah's apartment was sparkling clean, scrubbed and whisked and stuffed with Passover delicacies. And every item that contained one iota of *chometz*, or leavened grain, had been shoved into a heavy-duty plastic container and locked in the trunk of her car for the week, nestled under her Rollerblades. As she slipped behind the wheel and began the drive over to the community Seder at Sappho's Bar and Grill, Hannah cackled at the thought of perplexed archeologists from some future century unearthing her car in its present state. What would they make of the Amish pancake mix, the pot brownies, the whole-wheat spaghetti, and half-eaten box of Life cereal folded behind adult-sized in-line skates? Theologians and historians at the highest level of scholarly learning, now buoyed by digitized online databases of archeology, still barely understood the meaning of the Dead Sea Scrolls. Jewish ritual had survived, practiced over millennia, in part because mixed-marriage children like Hannah were willing to give up bread for a week, remembering the flight from slavery in Egypt. Yet Passover matzah still had to be explained anew in a store, which had sold it to at least three generations of Jewish college students and faculty.

If Jews carrying on tribal traditions in Christian America caused confusion at Safeway, Hannah wondered what future archaeologists and history detectives would conclude about the lesbian community she also belonged to in her lifetime. By now she had participated in as many lesbian rituals as Jewish ones. But almost no one was archiving lesbian culture. It had no synagogue, no great repository like the Cairo Geniza, just the Lesbian Herstory Archives in Brooklyn that occasionally sent Hannah newsletters, looking for donations.

What artifacts and evidence of hearty dyke life were being left behind for scientists to discover and puzzle over? How did lesbians get together and "worship"? Some futuristic scientist would conclude from evidence that lesbians partook of ritual drinking of alcohol at bars. They gathered in worship of women's music performers. They dressed up ritually in plaid flannel, and participated in sacred games like pool tournaments. Hannah laughed all the way to Sappho's, picturing mustachioed scholars with laser-point magnifying glasses bent over newly discovered burial mounds from the late twentieth century. The lost garbage underneath Isabel's bar alone would be a rich dig, yielding a battered copy of, say, Rita Mae Brown's *Rubyfruit Jungle;* old VHS tapes of lesbian films from the 1980s (*The Hunger, Personal Best, Lianna, Desert Hearts*); blue pool chalk, New Year's Eve decorations, unstapled copies of *Lesbian Connection,* the wrapper from a container of tofu, a forgotten softball jersey, bad butch cologne (*Millionaire, Coty Wild Musk, Axe, Nautica*), scratched Olivia albums and women's music cassettes. Somewhere in that burial mound would be Woody Simmons's banjo compositions playing and playing for all eternity to discover, and a pin that stated, *Well-Behaved Women Seldom Make History.* What would Hannah take with her if, like an Egyptian pharaoh, she brought her most prized possessions into her tomb at burial? What would that reveal about who she had been? Would her personal time capsule be more lesbian than Jewish? Probably. What did that say about her true tribe, her people?

We are what we take with us. We are what we leave behind.

The parking lot was jammed with Honda Civics, bumper-sticker-bearing trucks and motorcycles. If there was one event that drew the community together, it was the Seder. Isabel, who wasn't Jewish herself, somehow managed to provide all the ritual ingredients of the Seder plate from her own herb garden and other sources, festooning the long table in the bar's dining area with garlands, with thick stoneware carafes of wine and honey mead, even filling marked goblets with nonalcoholic brew for sober guests. Everything was gently arranged to welcome the many women who, though committed to celebrating the Jewish holidays, were now excluded from family gatherings back home because they were gay.

"*You* can come, but don't even think of bringing *that woman*," Karen's mother had hissed. "We'd love to see you. Without Brenda," Arlene's father made clear. Homophobia still seared its burning brand in this community, so that bitter tears were shed aplenty during holidays, enough to salt the water for the special Seder meal, enough to form the bitter herb required on the table. But Isabel erased that pain with gracious, loving touches, and the regulars at Sappho's were arriving in spring finery, with bags of wine and matzah, greeting each other with hugs and kisses.

Tonight the bar was especially crowded with Jewish lesbians from four surrounding towns, eager to reconnect through ancient ritual. They always used a special women's Haggadah for this occasion, one which named explicitly the courage of Jewish women as survivors, and the oppression and liberation of other peoples throughout history. The original ten plagues enumerated in Scripture were blood, frogs, lice, cattle disease, blight, boils, hail, locusts, darkness, and the slaying of the first born. But here at Sappho's, their feminist Seder named modern plagues: rape, war, starvation, sexism, racism and anti-Semitism, homophobia, ageism, the oppression of the disabled, classism, and environmental destruction. A special goblet designated as Miriam's well dominated the centerpiece, naming Miriam as important to Jewish survival as her brother Moses. For Miriam had brought life-giving water to the desert. *Mayim!*

Taking her seat at the set table, Hannah was briefly exasperated to see that Isabel had paired her with someone she didn't know. She never got to sit next to a cherished ex-lover, or someone in the community she had a little crush on, or anyone charismatic like that. It just wasn't fair, this burden of being single and thus nipped in somewhere convenient amid dynamic couples. Why was she always having to explain the meaning of Passover, and their special dyke Seder, to a one-time visitor? But this guest, at least, seemed very Jewish-looking—in the way Hannah wasn't. A lifetime of well-intended idiots praising her for not looking Jewish had long worked on Hannah's last nerve, secretly attracting her to women who really did look like the genuine article. Any woman with rich, olive skin and a great Semitic nose was guaranteed to make Hannah weak with desire. This woman had an enormous mane of curly dark hair and just the faintest hint of a beard, which Hannah didn't mind at all, as she was starting to sprout some middle-aged facial hair herself. She leaned over the table, so crowded with dishes that her sleeve unfortunately trailed across the Seder plate, and shouted above the buzz of conversations, "Hello. I'm Hannah."

"Rima." The woman spoke with a faint accent. She looked down, shyly.

Further pleasantries were interrupted by a complex rearrangement of bar stools and chairs. One seat always had to be set by the door for Alina, who, raised in an ultra-Orthodox community, had been abused by her rabbi as a girl and now deeply distrusted ritual. She sat with her back to the wall, an eye to escape, conflict etched on her otherwise handsome face. It was her role to open the door at a critical moment and welcome in not Elijah, but the spirit of Miriam. Two other women were having a commitment ceremony in connection with the Seder; they had brought a rainbow *chuppah* for their canopy, and gifts were being piled upon the bar. Hannah felt a pang of envy—would she ever, ever find a lasting love again?—and gratitude, as well. Though single this year, again, she was out and proud as a Jewish lesbian, welcome in her own home with any partner she might bring along, her childhood years unburdened by abuse or violations as Alina had experienced. Someone began to sing, and everyone took their seats, holding hands, voices joining in:

"Woman I am,
Spirit I am,
I am the infinite within my soul
I have no beginning and I have no end
Oh, this I am."

They lit candles, naming their female ancestors. First, the foremothers of Judaism: Sarah. Rebekah. Leah. Rachel. Bilchah. Zilpah. Eve. Lilith. Ruth. Naomi. Miriam. Dinah. Esther. Vashti. Judith. Deborah. Huldah. Then, their own mothers and grandmothers, and their journeys, reflecting the diversity of the guests that night at Sappho's.

"My mother Bella, my grandmother Teresa," said Marie. "They came over from Sicily, sick for days. Someone told them they wouldn't be admitted to this country because they found lice in their hair—yes, one of the original ten plagues!"

"My momma Louanne, my big momma Jessie, and all the Cajun aunties," added Letty. "They harvested herbs in the Louisiana swamps to survive each winter ..."

"Great-auntie Ruby who raised me. Thrown out of the county courthouse for trying to register to vote, had that scar on her shoulder all her life from where she landed on the bottom step."

In sign language, Cathy fingerspelled three generations of Deaf women who dared to have Deaf daughters.

"My mother, whose Hebrew name is Mashah," Hannah listed. "Daughter of Ruth, daughter of Rose, daughter of Rachel." The stranger across from her nodded and smiled.

They dipped parsley into the ceramic bowls of salt water

meant to symbolize their tears, broke the various matzahs (traditional, whole-wheat, gluten-free), and chanted: "This is the bread of affliction, which our foremothers made and ate in their hasty departure from Egypt. Let all who are hungry come and eat. Let all who are needy come and celebrate. Now we are few—next year may we be many. Now we are oppressed—next year, may we all be free."

Hannah passed a sheet of matzah over to Rima, and the service continued with the telling of the exodus from Egypt, the Hebrew women unable to wait for their bread to rise as they ran into the desert with dough on their backs hard-baking in the sun. Who had faith that the Red Sea would part for them? That, even with their bowls and pans of unleavened bread, their meager possessions, their babies tied around their hips and breasts, they would make that crossing and survive? Who had believed, and led them over, declaring that she would dance with the women on the other side, her musical instrument held high like a beacon? Miriam, they all murmured over the wine and the candles. Miriam.

They sang Laura Berkson's composition, "Miriam, it's gonna be a long journey."

Hannah saw the stranger's eyes grow wet. Then wetter—she was really weeping. Hannah found the feminist Seder moving, too, but it must mean something else to this woman. Tears were streaming down her face. They ran onto her scarf and then, Hannah noticed, they continued to run down onto the table, rather than being absorbed by the woman's dress. The table actually began to grow wet with Rima's tears. All of a sudden Rima reached across the table and grabbed Hannah's hand with her own watery one.

"Can you swim?"

And then, just as someone's teenage daughter began to read aloud from the Four Questions—why is this night different from all other nights? — the room filled up with water.

And the water was bitter, cold and heavy, and filled with women—women screaming and grabbing at one another; their bread pans rose off their backs and then sank, spilling half-baked matzos into the rushing waves. Fish and coral and reeds and bits of fishing net scraped against Hannah's panicked eyes as they opened and shut in absolute incomprehension.

I'm drowning. I'm drowning. She tried to steady her tumbling body, to gain some sort of footing on the sea bottom, if that's what it was; her feet were not shod but bare now, making contact with sharp coral. Then the childhood memory of numberless beach days in California, her father teaching her to ride a wave, sent Hannah pushing up toward the surface, waiting to feel the last wave pass over her head. She shot up into air and took breath. Other women's heads were there, too, all around her, bobbing, gasping, wailing, praying.

"Hanneleh, Hanneleh," Rima bellowed. "Help me." And instantly Hannah's old lifeguard training kicked in, even as she wondered. *Hanneleh! Only my grandmother ever called me that! That's a secret name! How could she know?* "Help Chava breathe," Rima directed. "Over there, look, now! Help Lilit breathe!" Hannah opened her mouth and breathed life into the woman named Chava. Then the woman named Lilit. Then another woman and another.

Then Rima's mouth was on her own.

It was a breath, but it was also a kiss. It was something Hannah couldn't even name. It was oxygen but it was clear water, too, not salt. She drank in life.

Then the water swept off her back and from beneath her belly like a turning, slumbering lover of gigantic proportions, and the women washed up onto hard-packed but saturated sand hills, their skirts and scarves dripping, braids trailing, chests heaving. Hannah found she was underneath Rima, pinned down by soft breasts. Something hard, though, lodged between those breasts, was cutting Hannah's flesh. A tambourine.

"I AM MIRIAM," said Rima, and the dry *wadis* of that ancient desert filled up with water at her words, and the land's

24

empty wells filled and dripped wet with new water, and Rima laughed and laughed. "Get up," she shouted. "You women. All you women! This is the other side. Get up and dance." And they danced *Mayim*. Water in the desert.

She must have passed out, briefly, from exhaustion, because when Hannah opened her eyes again the sun had set and most of the other women had moved past the hillside, erecting makeshift tents from scarves and palm fronds. She was lying on her back in a scooped-out gulley below what could only be described as an oasis: palm tree, pool of water, a bowl of fruit and dates, and millions of sparkling stars overhead. Miriam, Lilit and Chava were also lying on their backs under those stars, spread out in formation beside Hannah, their four heads nestled and touching at the center, their bodies extended in four directions. Camels chewed and moaned distantly.

Miriam stirred, sensing that Hannah had awakened, and touched her hand. "So you are the visitor to my Passover," Miriam whispered.

"Actually, I thought you were visiting mine," Hannah admitted.

"This is Chava whom we all know," Miriam introduced the woman to her left. "You call her Eve."

"Wow—*what is that* you smell like?" marveled Hannah.

"Apples," said Eve.

"And here, this is Lilit—Lilith, the angry one," laughed Miriam, patting the fourth woman in their formation. "The man-hater."

"I'm not! Everyone says that," Lilith snarled. "I just don't like being told what to do by men." A bolt of lightning suddenly slashed through the night air, splitting one of the nearby rocks in two.

"That was meant for me," sighed Eve.

"No, for me," said Lilith.

"No more! Everyone is safe tonight," Miriam interrupted.

And, rising to her bare feet, she approached the split rock and gingerly reached into the jagged interior, extracting what appeared to be a fist-sized crystal. "This is the memory of light, the divine spark, the start of something you still keep so keep this close," she told Hannah, handing her the gemstone, which pulsed and tingled briefly, then grew cool.

"I—thank you. I'm grateful enough we made it through that water," Hannah began to say, only to hear a murmuring that grew louder and louder like a swarm of bees humming—and the sound was *dayenu*, the Passover song of gratitude. She realized anything she might say now had already been said. Long, long ago. These were her genealogical, mythical foremothers. But why was Hannah here?

"I took you here," Miriam thundered as though reading Hannah's thoughts, "because I saw the other tribe in you. You lead one another through water out of love." She reached into her still-wet robe, and pulled out a tiny piece of matzah wrapped in a water-resisting sheet of papyrus. "This is what I kept hidden, if we had nothing left. This is the piece I saved for someone's child, if there was no miracle and no one else survived. And you call it—*afikoman*?"

Hannah understood. "We celebrate Passover by having the youngest look for the hidden piece of matzah. I always found it; I always know where it is, even now that I'm grown."

"It's yours then," said Miriam. "What you were looking for, what you always sought even as the tiniest hidden piece, and even so small its taste still satisfied you, is women's knowledge."

Yes, thought Hannah. "So I guess I'm here because I want to learn your survival stories and take them back to my people— my other tribe, as you put it—the women who love women, the outsiders in my time," she ventured, inwardly wondering, *How am I going to get back there? Wake up. This HAS to be some sort of Biblical hallucination. Another dose of Isabella's mystery wine.*

"Listen then. My brother, Moishe, the Lawgiver? He is going to come soon, with the rules for living." Miriam gazed moodily into the desert. "Everything will change. He will forbid goddess worship, our naming the She-who-came-before. He will make an abomination out of her—and an abomination of them," and she pointed with her brown, creased hand to Lilith and Eve, who were now rapturously embracing and kissing under an olive tree. "So why was this night different from all other nights? Because I saw you telling my story, the women's story. In your place you do not leave us out." Then Miriam broke the last surviving piece of matzah into even smaller portions, and both of them ate. Hannah felt her entire body tingling, velvety sensations scraping over her limbs. There was no longer any boundary between the sacred and the sensual; there was only a female genetic code strung together across her heritage. Whomever she chose to love in her own time, this was what she brought with her: a desert origin, the water in the desert, a Jewish woman's wetness. Impulsively, Hannah reached up to Miriam's face and kissed her, long and hard. Miriam did not resist.

Lilith and Eve wandered back over, interested. "Well, that is certainly forbidden," said Eve.

"What isn't?" Lilith snarled. "Mostly, anything that won't bring forth children."

"We'll be punished again. Oy! I can feel the cramps starting up," Eve lamented.

"No, you can't. Not yet. We still have time; this is our night. And you have something for our guest, don't you? Come sit. Come sit, my sisters," Miriam beckoned, and the stars were twinkling, dazzling, and then apples fell out of Eve's robe, one after the other. They looked startlingly like the lump of crystal Miriam had extracted from the split rock.

"I saved this women's knowledge," Eve explained. "From the tree no one remembers. Eat. Later they will make the apple a symbol of teachers. Tonight it's a meal for you, who came back to learn," and Lilith stood guard over them as Hannah feasted on apples.

"The first thing is that you have to push back against what men will say and do. Push back. Then push out what is real and true. I am the midwife; they have called me Puah, which means breath," said Miriam, "because I blow words of truth into the mother and the child is brought from her womb. The mother and I push together with breath and words. You have not had children but you have raised a thousand, with your breath," she smiled at Hannah, who thought: *Yes, my countless lectures. I've taught so many students women's history, breathing words across the aisles. And they called me pushy, blowhard, all those slurs for feminist. Am I a midwife, too?*

"Push back," said Miriam, and once again her voice was loud as thunder, and three stars twinkled out. "Push back against the patriarchs to come."

"Amen!" The table rocked against Hannah's knees; her eyes flew open; a square of matzah fell out of her mouth as she gasped. She was back at Sappho's Bar and Grill, surrounded by tipsy yet reverent friends on their fourth glass of wine at a lesbian Seder in her own time. Where was Rima? The mystery guest was gone. But at her place, an apple-shaped lump of crystal. "That's yours," nodded Isabel, bustling out of the kitchen annex with a tray of macaroons. "You found the *afikoman* yet again."

Chapter Three

Mother's Day

"Okay, Mom. I love you too. Call me after you see the podiatrist, okay? And please, go easy on the marijuana." Hannah held the phone—warm from being clenched to her left ear—for a few more seconds, wiggling her toes and grinning. Her mother, frustrated by arthritic foot pain after many years as a modern dance instructor, was now enjoying a medical marijuana prescription.

Well, *that* had not been a typical Mother's Day phone call, but was anything in Hannah's life normal this year? There was that first encounter, at the bar, with Sappho—if, indeed, that had really happened—and then a desert night with Miriam, too, during the most unforgettable Seder Hannah had ever attended. She had not told her mother about these incidents, dreading questions about her own sanity. She didn't want to speculate, analyze, break it down into Yes, It Happened or No, It's Not Possible. If her academic life had become sticky enough to pick up some magic dust, fine. Let it be.

Her thoughts turned from the pleasure of the Sunday morning conversation with her mom to the elaborate Sunday afternoon ahead: the graduation ceremony she had to attend on campus.

First, brunch. Knowing that her stingy university would serve just wine and cheese after the three-hour-long ritual, Hannah poured pancake batter onto the griddle and added spoonfuls of sliced banana and slivered almonds. She settled on Alaskan coffee to fortify her spirits. This should be a day of absolute matriarchy, she mused, with all rituals and events celebrating Woman, capital W. It was highly unusual for the university to schedule graduation on Mother's Day, an accident of calendar and convenience, and local business owners were ecstatic with double and triple orders for flowers. Every restaurant was booked either for Mother's Day lunch or graduation dinner, there were no balloons left to buy anywhere in town, and table centerpieces were going for a hefty markup. Hannah hoped that every graduate would take extra care to thank Mom throughout the afternoon ceremonies. And yet ... of the hundreds of college students receiving their diplomas later that day, how many had studied the *history* of their own foremothers, whose lives were conveniently not included in "the canon" of required learning?

Hannah shoveled in pancakes and coffee as she looked over the list of young women "commencing" from her own academic department. Only sixteen students were graduating with women's history degrees this May. Bowing to pressure from right-wing alumni and trustees, the university had dropped a requirement that all humanities students take at least one women's history class during their four years of study. Instead, they were encouraged (but not asked) to try a "gender" elective, such as Masculinities or Queering Fatherhood. Despite multiple waves of feminism, one could still earn a B.A. with no exposure whatsoever to women's history.

And even the women's studies majors received *bachelor's* degrees as proof of graduation.

Before she showered and dressed, Hannah cued up layers of feminist music to match her mood: Ova's "Who Gave Birth to the Universe?," Mosa Baczewska's "It's a Very Long Song That We Can Sing to Celebrate the Women of the World," Faith Nolan's "I, Black Woman," Ronnie Gilbert's "Mother's Day," Bitch and Animal's "Pussy Manifesto." *The mother. The body.* She rubbed some of her own mother's favorite lavender lotion on her arms and legs, still pale from the winter months of being shut

30

inside a classroom. Soon, there would be picnics, biking, Pride parades. She'd regain her Jewish tan, be olive-skinned again. For now, shaking off the academic hibernation of a school year was like stepping out of a cave and blinking at the promise of spring.

Now, what to wear? It hardly mattered, hidden under flowing black regalia; but Hannah felt her dykedom rising up, rebellious sap. Yes, she owned a dress. But she didn't have to wear it. Not today.

Her thoughts flickered unhappily to that day in the classroom when, as a younger professor in her third year of teaching, she vowed never again to wear a dress in front of students. It was during a disastrous, experimental first-year course inviting new students to write about the body and to debate reproductive rights. What a melee! Several male students assigned to the course by well-intentioned advisors were restless and rude, laughing at terms like "femicide," and swapping AIDS jokes. One young man, eventually expelled for acts of violence against women in his residence hall, scrawled an obscene drawing of Hannah on the attendance sheet she'd passed around. His crude sketch showed her in her favorite dress, being walked like a dog on a leash, her breasts spilling out and dragging on the ground. Hannah returned the next day in combat boots and trousers: survival gear, symbolically characterizing the rest of that challenging semester.

But, she reminded herself, one angry young man did not sum up a career teaching women's history. This was a day to celebrate her own devoted graduates, the ones who had daringly majored and minored in women's studies, whose loyalty and written work affirmed her purpose here on earth. Childless herself, Hannah had made these students her own children, pouring maternal energy into academic relationships. She brought cookies to class, worried about sick or absent students, sent little gifts and cards when someone won an internship or a job.

School and school and school again. No, she had not paused to have or raise children. She had, instead, raised activists. Graduation served as Hannah's own Mother's Day. This was her day

31

of pride in her young feminist progeny. (*Hadn't Miriam said so? But did that really happen?*)

Now, standing in front of her own long mirror—which, unlike the one at Sappho's Bar and Grill, did not reflect strange ghosts of women past—she considered graduation day jewelry. Definitely, the Venus of Willendorf pendant. Hannah plucked it on its long, light chain from the surface of her polished cedar dresser. This had been her own graduation gift, from her own mother, on the day she finally earned her Ph.D. The voluptuous Venus figure was shiny from having been rubbed and fondled absent-mindedly whenever Hannah wore it, the full belly of the ancient, faceless goddess now as smooth as glass.

Was it so much to want her students—hell, *all* students—to know that once upon a time, everyone worshipped a female deity?

As Hannah drove across town, she mentally reviewed the simple realities of pre-Christian goddess worship. The Venus of Willendorf! Someone had blundered into a cave in Austria in 1908 and discovered that limestone goddess "figurine," all breasts and hips and belly. No face; the artist, taking up chisel and rock back in 25,000 BCE, hadn't considered that feature important. Not in a time when children breastfed until they were five, when every human born looked to the mother as the creator of life, the feeder, the one who produced children and immediately provided them with sustenance. How had that association changed so permanently to a male God, the Father figure creating woman, and not only that, but creating her as the *second* sex? How had a female's ponderous flesh and belly, her reproductive enormity, come to be shamed as mere fat instead of sacred fertility? Why were so many of her students wracked by eating disorders, afraid of appetite, disdainful of curves?

Don't get angry. Don't get angry. It's Mother's Day. It's Graduation Day.

Hannah peeled off her hard folding chair as the final row of graduated seniors exited the stage, holding aloft diplomas and beaming. Three hours of speeches by male provosts and deans, three hours of "God, He" invocations by campus ministry! A stiff drink at Sappho's Bar and Grill would be her reward in just about forty-five minutes. She did love hearing the names of her own hard-working students announced over the public address speakers: *Terry Wong, Women's Studies. Emerald Granger, Women's History. Elena Gonzalez, Women's History.* Those students would now come up to her with hugs, with thanks and gladness. It was the parents who were so unpredictable at these occasions.

Hannah didn't know who might yank her chain this time, but there was always some uptight parent, usually a father, who felt compelled and authorized to mock her field. "Well, we tried to talk her out of it, but she chose women's history," this father would say, right to Hannah's face. "Now she'll never get a job. Can you find her one?" Or: "We didn't have, you know, women's history classes when I was here. We had real subjects: econ, philosophy . . ." "A waste of tuition in my opinion, this gender thing, but I know she had fun in your classes. Well, now she'll have to get serious." Even the kinder or empathetic remarks were psychologically draining and stressful. There was the mother who had whispered to Hannah at a parents' brunch that winter: "In my time we knew about feminism, but we couldn't bring it into the sorority house. No women's studies books on the table, especially not when gentlemen came to call. I read about Emma Goldman in the bathroom."

She needed the bathroom herself. The nearest one was in the Science building, but Hannah automatically vetoed that comfort station, knowing its history. When the university was constructed, no women's bathrooms were added to the math, science, or engineering halls, on the assumption that no women would ever be admitted or, if grudgingly admitted, would never major in the "hard" sciences. When the 1960s brought in women, when the 1970s brought in feminism, when the 1980s and '90s brought in computer science and women demanding access to STEM fields, the embarrassed university contrived a ladies' room out of an old broom closet in the Science wing. Hannah preferred to avoid an environment of second-class citizenship on this day.

But here came a dad. She sensed the blossoming confrontation, like a person allergic to cats involuntarily responding to that first hint of dander floating spore-like in the air. He strode up in his pressed chinos, nodded, and indicated her faculty robes. "So. You're a professor here. What do you teach?"

Here it comes, Hannah thought, scrambling for her academic party manners. "Well, sir, happy graduation day to you. I teach several women's studies courses here at the university. For instance—"

He interrupted her, swirling the chardonnay in his plastic wineglass. "There's *women's studies* here? How come there's no *men's* studies?"

Hannah, practiced at this sort of opening salvo, chirped, "Sir, every other subject taught here, every other major, is men's studies, you see." She was calm, but the heat of being once again forced to defend her life's work—on what should be a day of scholarly triumph, closure, culmination—was bringing on yet another hot flash. She pulled off her academic robe, flinging it over her left arm. It caught on her Venus of Willendorf necklace, and she could feel the chain tug and then break, slipping down the back of her blouse.

Now the dad was taking in Hannah's pinstripe pants, vest and silk shirt, which were a marked contrast to the sleek, shoulder-revealing dresses worn by nearly every other female at the event. "So I guess *your* favorite woman in history is Joan of Arc," he sneered.

Hannah thought of that moment in February when she was sipping one of Isabel's drinks at Sappho's, and briefly saw burnt Joan seated beside her at the bar in the mirror's dim reflection. Refusing to take the bait—the man clearly knew Joan was a cross-dresser—she answered truthfully, "Yes, I teach Joan and

34

Sappho, Alice Paul, the Irish pirate Grace O'Malley, Sojourner Truth, and of course the Venus of Willendorf, whose image I wore today at graduation. I also teach the history of the All American Girls Baseball League—"

"Yeah. That lasted for what, a year?"

"No, sir; the league extended from 1943 all the way through 1954."

For ten minutes, it went on like that, like a torturous badminton rally. He tested and tested her with sarcastic but educated bait, looking for a crack in her armor. She remained as dignified as possible, feeling the sweat trickle down her breasts and the Venus necklace slipping, slipping down her back, past her underwear, probably falling all the way down onto the ground. She didn't dare move, lest she trample on or lose her own graduation necklace. He had metaphorically yanked her chain, and her chain was literally underfoot now, being trampled.

And finally he was through with her. With a half-smile, he raised his glass and said, "Well, some feminists are very pushy, and I don't like that. But . . . I guess we needed feminism." As Hannah took in his intentional use of the past tense, *needed*, he added one parting shot: "I am an obstetrician." Then he walked away to join his wife and son.

She stood there, reeling. So he'd earned his son's tuition by "helping" women give birth yet it never occurred to him that women created life, and thus the world? Or that women's storylines as mothers had shaped all living people? Or that the history of how and when women's fertility might have been celebrated in an era before his own could be compelling knowledge, taught to thinking minds?

She squatted down, angry hands seeking her broken Venus of Willendorf necklace. She'd go right to the jeweler now, before stopping in at Sappho's, and have the chain repaired. No, wait; it was Sunday. Mother's Day. Everything was closed. Damn it.

The ground was moist and warm. She could smell mud where thousands of elegantly and not-so-elegantly shod feet had crushed the neatly mown grass as families raced for good seats from which to cheer their graduates. She pushed her hand through the damp grass stubble—ah, there!—and closed her fingers around her silver chain. But as she pulled it up toward her hot neck, someone, or something, just underneath that earth pulled just as hard. With an *oof!* of surprise, Hannah fell facedown onto the ground and melted through it to the other side.

She was in a cave. That much was clear. Very little light afforded much more information, but the stone walls, dripping moisture, streaked with recent painted images, pressed in around her. An overwhelming smell of animal life, and human life as well, filled her nose and eyes—a scent of wet hair, sweat, warm milk, fresh blood, old urine, matted wool, babies, and something else more fecund. Hannah was not alone.

There was a woman there. Lying on her side on an animal skin, heaving with the grip of labor pains, a giant body pushed and moaned and shuddered. Hannah approached, terrified, yet drawn to this great stranger. No matter which angle she approached from, she could not see a face. But all around her on the walls were drawings of women's bodies. Pregnant. Nursing. Holding infants. Dancing.

And now, just beyond the cave entrance, Hannah could see dozens and then hundreds and then thousands of eyes, watching. Waiting. It looked like the vigil of an entire community, an entire tribe, awaiting the birth. Some of the half-clad figures were holding small statues of pregnant women, of mothers, of mothers breastfeeding. She heard low chanting.

There is more respect for the motherline here than in my own time. I am in the birthing chamber of the Venus of Willendorf.

Something was wrong, or stalled, or difficult with this birth. Yet everything depended on the birth of a daughter, who represented the future of the tribe; Hannah understood this. There was something she was supposed to do. There was a reason she was here. Water trickled down the cave wall, and Hannah suddenly thought of water in a desert: *Miriam. I am Miriam's well. I am the traveler with Miriam's knowledge. Miriam is still in the future, but I am from the future too. There is no time. There is no time to waste. This is the midwifing of the world, the daughter-naming hour.*

The baby would be the next mother goddess to this nascent civilization. If she emerged, if she lived. Tentatively, Hannah approached the fiercely puffing mother. "Push," she said. "Push." What language was right for such urgent instruction? English? Hebrew? German? Which words did Miriam breathe to the laboring women? Would song be better? Hannah thought of the composer Kay Gardner, who had suggested there was an elemental female sound, a note, an opening of vowels—that the ancient word for God was simply voices breathing a-e-i-o-u. A woman in labor would howl in any alphabet as she herself became God, the creator and giver of life.

"Just keep pushing!" Hannah shrieked, and the *sh* of *push* became a wind, and the wind a hammock of breath blown forward, and the infant crowned, the very beginning of a new daughter's hair emerging from the now-open yoni. And now the mothering woman half-rose from her posture of contraction, and to Hannah's terror she was faceless, though wild-haired and live and breathing. And from the blurred non-face came this blurred answer: "You. Also. Push."

"What did you say?" Hannah whispered, and the breath of ages came back to her again in her own language, stilted with effort. "You." A breath. "You. Pushy. Woman. You. Keep. Pushing." Then silence. Hannah pressed closer, fearful of looking at that huge faceless being, but also fearful something had gone wrong.

The infant was pulled forward, handed to and immediately suckled by two waiting mothers, while a third woman with breast milk trickling thinly used a sharp stone to cut the umbilical cord.

And as Hannah watched, as the stone cut through the cord, the giant cave-filling mother turned to stone herself.

She was pulled out of the cave by many warm hands. Further confounding Hannah, the vigil-keeping tribe now melted into the recognizable features of her former students, both male and female. They lifted her above their heads and passed her forward, as if she were crowd surfing at a rock concert. She was aware that below her were the first women's studies students she had ever taught, as a graduate teaching assistant years and years ago. Then the star students from that tough first course on reproductive rights. Forward into her own time she rolled, over class after class, graduate after graduate. Frances, who had died young. Lisa, who became a top United Nations lawyer for global women's rights. Andi, the sculptor. How she had pushed them to work harder, to write better, to read more, to speak up and act and advocate!

I am a rock star. I am surfing Neolithic feminism. The rock is the mother and the rock is the Neolithic, the New Stone Age. The children of the daughter born today will worship the Goddess and carve her image and leave it, forever, inside that cave. "Push," whispered the students of Hannah's past. "You pushed us. You stay pushy. You keep pushing."

"Dr. Stern. Are you okay?" Three of today's freshly minted graduates stood over Hannah, their dark mortarboards blocking the sun. Manicured hands reached down to pull Hannah up from the damp grass. "Oh, that's a shame! Did you break your necklace?" Terry Wong, that year's star student, took the Venus pendant and chain and carefully placed them into the small box that had earlier held her class graduation ring. "There! That should keep it safe, at least until you get it fixed. Wow, I've seen you wear that in class a thousand times! I guess today's the last time I'll ever see you decked out in your goddess gear."

"God, Terry, are you going to start crying again?" The other students smiled at Hannah. Terry beckoned to an older woman whose scarf shimmered with blue and gold strands. "Dr. Stern, this is my mother. She wanted to meet you." Hannah tried to remain steady on her feet as the proud mom introduced herself and expressed thanks for Hannah's mentoring. "We're very proud that Terry chose this major—her other mom and I," and now a second woman came forward to shake Hannah's still-trembling hand. "It's a moment we never thought we'd see or celebrate. We had so much difficulty just bringing her into the world . . ."

"Mama! Dana! Not that story again," Terry groaned.

"Just such a difficult birth," the co-mom reminisced, ruffling the hair of her healthy, now-grown daughter. "Thank God we had that visiting woman doctor, because we had no legal rights as a couple in those days."

"Right, they wouldn't let Dana stay with me in the birthing room, or touch me or help me; and I was desperate. I had to push, and push, and push . . . Yes, Terry, it's all worth it today. All worth it to see you so grown up. And a women's history graduate!"

They stood around her, beaming.

She parked shakily in the lot behind Sappho's and entered through the back door, the hall that emptied into the bar's open space. Like tumbling down the birth canal. She wanted that feeling, now, on Mother's Day. A party was in progress, of course, with local lesbian moms and their progeny snacking on cookies and milk (and stronger beverages for some of the mothers) as Isabel played soundtracks in celebration of motherhood. Hannah put the box containing her broken necklace on the bar and took a cup of milk from the party platter, surprised by its odd flavor—perhaps another one of Isabel's mystic herbal concoctions? —until Melissa shouted "Wait! Hannah! That's my *breast milk*. I pumped it out for Jiji earlier. I'm so sorry, I forgot all about it!"

"Hey, professor!" welcomed Letty, her arms draped around a tough-looking grown daughter and two grandkids. "School's over for the year, right? Graduation day up at campus? Yeah, baby! You're done. You can come out of your cave now and join us." But

Letty's kind words "join us" sounded, to Hannah, like "Venus," and she looked down at her feet, where the rough clay of an actual cave still stuck to her damp shoes. Isabel looked, too, and saying only "Wipe your feet," she handed Hannah a small towel with a smile. An instant later, when Hannah had cleaned her shoes, she lifted her head and saw that Terry's little ring box had popped open like a gesture of proposal, on the bar. Inside, her silver necklace chain was perfectly intact, the links in a solid circle, and the Venus pendant polished as if new.

Chapter Four
Birthday Week

"I'm going to England next month," Isabel said. "My annual vacation time." Hannah knew that Iz took only ten days off each year, the only time she felt she could close the bar: mid-May. That was right at the point when all the university students had graduated or cleared out of town for summer, but before the many festivities of Memorial Day and Pride Month, which brought in the regulars and locals. Isabel paused, then looked up at Hannah: "I have a two-for-one flight, and I know it's your birthday that week. Would you like to accompany me to London?"

Would she! Dozens of emotions played across Hannah's face: surprise, gratitude, thrill, panic, and anticipation. "You look like one of those children's flipbooks, where thumbing the pages speeds up the character's changes of expression," laughed Isabel.

"Yes, you have animated me," Hannah teased back. But it had been a dream of hers for so long: ENGLAND. To walk in the streets that gave birth to the English language, which after all was her medium, her literary tongue, her wordlife. This was a particularly important birthday, too: FORTY-FIVE, and she'd had no plans, still being single. Now the plan peeled open around her like a tantalizingly sweet onion. A pilgrimage to Radclyffe Hall's grave.

Once, doing research in San Francisco's gay and lesbian archives during a Pride Month trip, Hannah had been allowed to look at an old letter Radclyffe Hall had mailed to another lesbian author. Sealed in a protective sheet and kept in a climate-controlled archive room, the letter was paired with its original envelope, and Hannah had carefully copied down the return address: 37 Holland Street, Kensington W8, London. Later she'd written the long-dead lesbian novelist a long letter, expressing clumsily what Hall's life had meant to her, and impulsively mailed it to the London address with no return address of her own so that it couldn't be sent back. *I wrote to a ghost*, thought Hannah. *Now I can set flowers on her grave.*

"I'll be with you as far as Heathrow," Iz was saying. "Then I have a side trip to meet up with some mixologists—sort of a retreat for those of us in the bar-wench profession." She smiled as she wiped down the bar with a clean towel. "I'll let you prowl in London for a few days, then I'll be back and meet up with you for a night or two of fun before we fly back."

"Oh. Sure. Are you going to another part of England? Some brewery village?"

"No, somewhere and something else," said Isabel, and with no further comment she handed Hannah a slim folder containing a plane ticket.

Highgate Cemetery was green and glowing that May afternoon. If there were any pilgrims seeking the grave of Karl Marx, the most famous permanent resident of Highgate, they weren't in evidence. At least, Hannah saw no cluster of day-tripping social-ists as she alighted from the London bus. But almost immediately she found herself in an argument with the grim attendant at the front entrance, who demanded an enormous admission fee for the "group tour."

"I'm really fine just walking through on my own," Hannah tried to explain, thinking, *I'd rather put out my eyeball with a*

shrimp fork than join a tour group for my secret moment of homage.
But the matron snarled, "Ye can't poke about on yer own. We
can't have it, visitors tramping up and down. Ye stick with the
guide and no wandering off the path or it's out yer go, see?" So
Hannah presented the right number of pounds, and only after
receiving a stamped admit ticket remembered to ask, "Will the
tour take us to the tomb of Radclyffe Hall? That's who—that's
the site I've come to see."

"No promise," snarled Matron.

Obviously grave desecrations by cranks, and the risk of
damage or graffiti from vandals, could only be avoided by sen-
sible restrictions on all visitors, Hannah realized. But the meek
young man who led their eventual small party to historic
tombs responded to Hannah's desperate pleas with "Right.
Then. This is the tomb of Radclyffe Hall, a famous lady writer.
Quite controversial really." He wiped his sweating pate with a
pocket handkerchief, and then turned to the next tomb up the
path.

It was too much. She'd come all this way. No: she'd *come out*
all this way. "Lady writer"? Hall had to be spinning in her tomb.
"Sir," Hannah interrupted, "I'd like to add a few words about this
one. I'm a women's history professor, myself. If you wouldn't
mind." "Ooh!" one of the other patrons in the tour group
exclaimed, and their guide gave a quick, reluctant nod.

So Hannah launched into the familiar homage she knew by
heart from class lecture notes, used over and over every fall, every
spring, every year.

"Okay, so this is the tomb of the *famous lesbian author,* Radclyffe Hall, whose novel *The Well of Loneliness* became the central
lesbian classic of the twentieth century," she began. "Published
in 1928, the book was instantly banned and vilified in the English
press. It received the same treatment across the pond in America.
Obscenity trials painted the book as dangerous to youth, and one
judge famously said, 'I would rather give a healthy young woman
a phial of prussic acid than this novel.' The heroine, Stephen
Gordon, is a rich and privileged butch girl forced to leave her

43

family's estate, who falls in love with a rather clueless young woman against the backdrop of World War I.

"Lesbians across many generations have found the book disappointing, due to its self-loathing portrait of an outcast 'invert.' It's not at the top of the list of what you'd call Gay Pride literature, and there sure aren't any descriptive sex scenes, for all that the book was a scandal. The one line that left critics gasping was something like 'and that night, they were not divided.' But overall, millions of women smuggled paperback editions home, to read at least one in-print testament to lesbian love. And the book raised questions about everything from homophobia to disinheritance to cross-dressing to lesbians' roles as ambulance drivers on the wartime French front. So some of the most enlightened feminist educators and social scientists of the pre-World War II era read and debated the book. It trickled down to curious readers of all backgrounds and ethnicities."

She swallowed. "Like many a young lesbian, I read *The Well of Loneliness* during my coming-out period, although by that time there were women's history classes and lesbian literary critics interpreting the book for me. I understood that, for all its flaws, this once-banned book was part of my cultural inheritance as an English-speaking lesbian. That's why I've traveled to Hall's gravesite today—to pay homage to her—on my birthday," she finished weakly.

There were a few automatic mumbles of "many happy returns." Other members of the tour group had grown restless by now; a few looked downright embarrassed and resentful, although one tweedily dressed woman was taking notes on a green file card. But the guide put a trembling hand on Hannah's forearm. "You know, Miss, this tomb is indeed the most visited spot in High-gate. Young ladies regularly leave bouquets here. I'm grateful for the expertise you shared. Quite frankly, I'm not up to it."

"I didn't mean to show you up," Hannah apologized. "It's just that I came all this way only to see her tomb, and worried that we'd pass it all too quickly."

Her guide regarded her from behind stiff brown-rimmed eyeglasses. "Well . . . it's in violation of our rules, really, but I see you're sincere. If I can trust you to behave yourself," he added with a surprising amount of twinkle, "would you like a few moments alone at this tomb? I have to insist that you rejoin the group within five minutes. No more than that. Agreed?"

"Agreed!" Hannah couldn't believe her luck. *Yes! Whoopee! Alone with Hall.* The instant the guide moved tactfully away (the other tourists having scattered far ahead), Hannah fumbled both her journal and camera out of her knapsack and began wildly sketching and photographing Hall's tomb. There wasn't much to see: an imposing rusty door, with a tenderly inscribed plaque attributed to Hall's longtime partner Lady Una Troubridge: "I will but love thee more." Hannah made a quick pencil rubbing of this plate, moving so fast that she accidentally tore a bit of paper from her journal.

Then she noticed the keyhole. *There was a keyhole in Radclyffe Hall's tomb.* Whatever for? Who went in and out? Karl Marx and the other ghosts of Highgate? But they wouldn't need keys. The matron, the shy tour guide? Did they come in and tidy the dust of a lesbian life? Drink with Hall, after work? Her mind raced through the macabre possibilities. But the tour guide was waiting. Quickly, before she could change her mind, Hannah wrote on the scrap of torn journal paper *Radclyffe, you are not forgotten,* and she rolled it into a slender joint-like arrow and pushed it through the keyhole. Into the tomb.

A rush of cold, cold air blew back into her face. Hannah dropped to her knees. It was a still, warm day in May with no wind. But the icy blast came from the other side of that tomb keyhole, a shift in atmosphere and form that seemed to whisper, *I received your note. I am reading it now.*

Gasping, drenched in cold sweat, Hannah ran to rejoin the tour group, the guide giving her a look that said it all: *Now do you understand what we have going on here?* She looked back. There was nothing to indicate any tinkering with the tomb. As promised, she had not disturbed the site—just, apparently, the atmosphere.

Isabel's voice on the other end of the phone sounded amused but not too surprised as Hannah spewed the story of her afternoon at Highgate. "Look, there's a party at a bar. A bold Radclyffe Hall theme tonight, actually, so I knew you'd be interested. It's a literary event, everyone joining in a group reading of *The Well of Loneliness*. Perfect for your birthday night if you don't have other plans." She knew Hannah had no other plans. And it was their last night in London.

The bar was called Lady Una's. Motorcycle after motorcycle (and a few Rolls Royces, too) purred up to dismount party guests, the riders all dressed in the style of Radclyffe Hall, top hats and monocles replacing crash helmets and chaps tonight. All of a sudden Hannah realized this was a fancy-dress party where every invited guest was in a prescribed costume except Hannah herself: the clumsy, underdressed American on the trail of Hall's legacy. Whether the odd setup was Isabel's idea of a joke, or a sort of present for Hannah's birthday, she wasn't sure. She only knew that she was caught alone in Kensington W8 London wearing her Lucy travel pants, her green walking shoes, and an old polo shirt that felt unbearably out of style.

As she stood uncertainly on the kerb (and it's called kerb here, she reminded herself) the bar door cracked open and two Radclyffes spilled out, arguing. They glared at Hannah, who was blocking their path. Then, to her astonishment, a real horse and carriage appeared out of nowhere, and the more feminine of the two said to her companion "Really, John, I told you our driver would be here," and they disappeared into a musty, curtained compartment.

Then Isabel was in the doorway, greeting Hannah with a beautiful, broad smile and a soft string bag containing everything necessary for a Radclyffe Hall costume. She drew Hannah inside. A huge crowd of dapper, rowdy lesbians had assembled for a staged reading of the entire *Well of Loneliness,* in the style of booklovers' readings of James Joyce on Bloomsday, or Robbie

Burns night celebrations. "This only happens once every few years," Isabel was explaining, "and I knew it would correspond to your birthday this time. Everyone's waiting for you." "Everyone," in this case, included several of Hannah's favorite Brit writers, lesbian icons she recognized despite their varied and authentic Radclyffe Hall drag. Sarah Waters had her arm around Jeanette Winterson, who was goosing Emma Donoghue.

How does she do it? Hannah marveled, watching Isabel's bar wench gravitas cross cultures into another country altogether. Then she recalled how, back home at Sappho's Bar and Grille, Isabel kept books on lesbian culture and specialty bottles from global lesbian bars behind the counter. Why couldn't a London bar have a souvenir from Sappho's? As Hannah pulled the tweed blazer around her shoulders, admiring both its heft and its weft, the long dark bar packed with Radclyffe Hall look-alikes cheered and roared approval. Then Hannah saw that behind the counter, where at home Isabel kept a first-edition copy of *The Well of Loneliness*, this dear and mysterious pub called Lady Una's kept a bottle of American apple brandy—and a hardcover copy of a small-press textbook on lesbian history by one Dr. Hannah Batsheva Stern.

One of her own published books.

Tears sprang to her eyes. She would never be Radclyffe Hall, never host a literary salon beyond the humble state university classroom where she lectured and snarled, but somehow her research was being circulated—and read. *Known. Here!*

The Radclyffes shouted and stamped their welcome, some calling out "Author!" and others toasting her with whisky and ale. "Many Happy Returns!" "It's because you've honored our Radclyffe Hall in your classes and your writing," explained one wispy drunk lass. "Paid homage at her tomb, today, now didn't you?" another praised. "And you teach her life story," nodded a severely cropped megadyke in tie and tails, offering Hannah a slice of birthday cake.

But then the serious purpose of the evening resumed, and the little stage was set with a reader's high stool and lectern, candlelit and ringed with folding chairs. "Your turn, Hannah," said the Radclyffe-of-ceremonies at the mic, handing Hannah a leather-bound first edition. "Page one, have a go."

"Don't fuck it up, now, Yank!" another Radclyffe bellowed good-naturedly from the bar.

She read the first page, blushing, hearing breaths and bottle-openings and the clink of drink around her, hands adjusting monocles, the smack of stolen kisses, pages flipping, pub grub passing around with forks for cake. "Now read a *favorite* page," instructed burly Radclyffe-at-the-mic. "And don't give us that same old 'that night they were not divided' part; every baby dyke picks that. We know she did it—in fiction as in life. No argument. But find some short passage that spoke to you and only you." So Hannah turned automatically to the paragraph she always read aloud to her own students:

And now quite often while she waited at the stations for the wounded, she would see unmistakable figures—unmistakable to her they would be at first sight, she would single them out of the crowd as if by instinct. For as though gaining courage from the terror that is war, many a one who was even as Stephen, had crept out of her whole and come into the daylight, come into the daylight and faced her country: 'Well, here I am, will you take me or leave me?' And England had taken her, asking no questions—she was strong and efficient, she could fill a man's place, she could organize too, given scope for her talent. England had said: 'Thank you very much. You're just what we happen to want . . . at the moment.'

There was silence after that. Then someone said, "There's gay-dar for you, in 1918." Another voice called, "Valour." The close-packed audience buzzed and wept. Some applauded. And Hannah saw one older woman fingering a medal on her breast. The red poppy.

It was too much. No birthday had ever been better. She mentally ranged through hideous or merely disappointing birthdays from age three upward, a catastrophe of humiliating images, some appallingly recent. The time she'd thrown up on the class-mate she'd expected to seduce. The time her date broke up with her and left her by the side of the road with no underwear. The carrot cake that made everyone sick. The guest who wanted all of Hannah's friends to boycott the hotel where they were heading to dance. The old boyfriend who showed up, stoned on Ecstasy. The fire in the kitchen stove that sent two terrified mice blundering over her mother's legs. This made up for it all. How had Isabel pulled it off? Why was she being so good to Hannah?

Embarrassed by her own display of emotion, Hannah pushed through the applauding dykes to the rear of the bar, fervently hoping for a bathroom stall in which to blow her nose and compose herself. Another Radclyffe Hall lookalike smiled and nodded to her as Hannah barreled into the loo and, observing Hannah's crimson face, extended a perfectly starched handker-chief from a blazer pocket. "Here, Miss."

"Sorry," Hannah sniffled, abruptly remembering that London's better public venues often hired a ladies' washroom attendant and that, having left her wallet and passport with Isabel, she now had no money in the pockets of her own costume. "I . . . don't have any change for the toilet."

The Radclyffe, amused, reached into another pocket and brought out a handful of coins Hannah had never seen before. Seeing her confusion, the handsome woman said "An American, is it? That's a ha'penny, that's a tuppence, that's threepence."

"Man, you went all out," Hannah blurted, admiring the coins long vanished from England's updated currency system. "You even dressed in the *change* Radclyffe would have carried around." But the woman regarded her with probing, hooded eyes, and the temperature in the bar bathroom abruptly dropped to the chill of a tomb's air as the stranger dipped long fingers into yet another pocket and slowly, slowly drew out the slip of paper Hannah had pushed into Hall's tomb earlier that day.

It was unmistakable. It was Hannah's handwriting. It still bore

49

the creases from being rolled like a joint and shoved through a slender tomb keyhole.

"You wrote to me twice," said the real Radclyffe Hall, "both times knowing I could not possibly write back, for all I am is temperature and dust, no longer temperament and lust." And then she smiled. "But keep trying. For as you read aloud just now from my old pages, we still recognize one another, do we not?" She leaned one hand lightly on Hannah's shoulder, and the icy breath of tomb surrounded them. Hannah, suspended in disbelief, panicking, thought to herself, *But I can't kiss the dead*, though she dimly recalled somehow making love with shimmering figments of Miriam and Eve and Lilith at some recent Passover Seder, and hadn't that been the impossible made real? Could there be a livelier birthday gift than making out with the ghost of Radclyffe Hall? But then wouldn't Lady Una's ghost haunt her forever? These thoughts were interrupted by Hall's competent writing hand, which began stroking history and savvy into Hannah, soon fiercely pushing pressure into her velvet costume breeches, a cold pressure of wartime and rejection and scandal and superiority and ink that grew to a spread of heat at its circling point, and Hannah smelled good horses, polished leather, men's cologne, the threads of costly hatbands, old tobacco, and the secret hidden sweat of one of history's greatest butches, and Hannah felt the impossible waves of a ghost-given orgasm start to unfold, and Hall was saying, "They all hate me now. They say the book depresses them, that it's full of self-loathing. They all want other writers now, the young and the tutors alike. They hate me now, as they did then, but you—you keep assigning me, and keeping me alive—and if they hate you, I will haunt them. Remember that. Write your truth, as I did, and when the critics lash you, as they will, know that I will haunt them; until they read you more—"

Then Hannah heard herself quote from Hall's own letters, breathing into the older woman's elegant neck her famous words: "'I do not like notoriety, it embarrasses me and makes me feel shy, but I realize that it is the price I must pay for having intentionally come out into the open, and no price could ever be too great in my eyes—Nothing is so spiritually degrading or so undermining of one's morals . . .'"

"—As living a lie, as keeping friends only by false pretences," finished Hall, and pressed again into Hannah, whispering in her ear, "Now. Write *this* down, my dear."

The toilet flushed, and Isabel came out, adjusting the tie of her Radclyffe suit. She looked at Hannah standing there, swaying, moaning, holding onto nothing, and gently said, "Love, you might want to wipe that graveyard dust off your rented boots," and exited the bathroom. Hannah opened her eyes to find the bathroom mirror steamed over in dripping streaks, with one long handprint that was not Hannah's slowly evaporating. And clutched in Hannah's own chilled hand was something cool and slim. Where had that come from? It was a fountain pen.

Seduced by the lesbian past, she thought. *Happy birthday to me.*

Chapter Five
Memorial Day

Hannah woke up smiling. School was over until fall, the air turning lush but not too warm yet, and Memorial Day weekend loomed. That was a special holiday for the regulars at Sappho's: not a celebration of the dead but of the living, although bar regular Shoni often set up a traditional sweat lodge to honor female warrior ancestors. The weekend focus was an annual campout at the property of two women who had built their yurt-style cabin retreat on several wooded acres just outside of town. The cabin was just luxurious enough (glass doorknobs, a flush toilet) to reassure the anxious, who slept inside; the outdoor setting just wild enough (no Internet reception, hawks and fox cubs) to satisfy the working women who couldn't afford a more expensive "nature" getaway. Everyone brought sleeping bags and partied long into the night, enjoying a barbecue, campfire songs, s'mores, Isabel's signature cocktails (or, if preferred, cheap wine coolers). Those woods had seen their fair share of spontaneous hookups, over the years. Janey and Amy had a cozy treehouse fort, built over the site of an old house foundation, and one year Hannah had spent the night making passionate love in that treehouse with a ruddy pest control manager named Flick.

When Hannah arrived on Friday afternoon, she made sure to sign up for the Saturday morning sweat lodge, which required that any participants stay clean and sober for twenty-four hours beforehand. Content to take in chocolate squares and gooey marshmallows as her only stimulants for the first night, she headed down to the campfire circle. There, the welcoming scent of woodsmoke mingled with spring blossoms, damp grass, and burnt graham crackers, with a faint undercurrent of mothballed sleeping bags and after-workout butch cologne splashed on buff limbs. Hannah's arrival had apparently interrupted a mild argument about the correct observance of the holiday.

"I stopped to put flowers on the grave of the unknown woman soldier," Moira was explaining. "And I'll probably ride in the parade on Monday with the other female vets. Got the bike tricked out, but will any of youse be there? Yvette? Dog? You know, you guys—it *is* Memorial Day weekend." Everyone looked down uncomfortably. Yvette started to say something, but Joanna shoved a marshmallow into her mouth.

"Huh! Did I say something wrong?" Moira stretched her legs toward the campfire, although it was a very warm day. "Did you know that Janey and Amy have some Civil War history right in their backyard here? Letty's grandkids found it."

"Come on, this is upstate *New York*," Dog protested.

"Yeah, and you're sitting right on the map of the Underground Railroad. Where do you think escaping slaves headed to? If not here, through here, to Canada. Where do you think Sojourner Truth began her life? Enslaved in *this state*." Moira reached for the bag of chocolate squares, tossing a handful to Hannah; one fell onto a burning log and melted dramatically, with a hiss of rich dissolving sugars. "I know, I know, Yvette and Hannah think all women should be pacifists and never take up arms or fight in uniform. But if you knew you would be sent to free women from slavery, wouldn't you sign up? I know I would have. Over in Bosnia, where they sent me as a peacekeeper resettling women from all those rape camps, I thought I could *be* a freedom train. For someone. That's all I'm saying."

"I don't think women should be passive in the face of slavery and genocide, if that's what you mean," Hannah heard herself join in. "I know women passed as men and went to war in the American Revolution, and the Civil War, and there was an all-women's battalion in Russia in World War I, the Battalion of Death. And there's Joan of Arc and even Hannah Senesh, who I'm named for, who parachuted into Nazi territory to rescue Jews. You know I teach this stuff." She turned to the other women. "I had Moira in as a guest lecturer during Women's History Month. They loved her."

"So, historian—would you fight? If you had to?" Moira waited. Hannah looked around the now-silent circle. She could hear Yvette chewing, Letty wheezing.

"I would fight like a historian," Hannah answered at last. "Like Rose Valland. She was the curator at the Louvre Museum who kept coded secret lists of what the Nazis were stealing—great art, the treasures of France. Just a mousy little woman no one paid attention to, who helped the French resistance. She helped recover some, but not all, of the art collections the Nazis stole from museums and from Jewish families. And without firing a single bullet, she was awarded the French Legion of Honor and even the Presidential Medal of Freedom from the U.S. And there was that New Zealander, Nancy Wake, the courier no Nazis could capture. The Gestapo called her the White Mouse." She took a swig of limeade, thinking: *I bet I could have done something like that. My best friend and I used code to pass love notes to each other in tenth grade. We would have been hassled and shunned otherwise. Every lesbian learns the art of concealment, espionage, coded letter-writing. I wish the students I'm teaching now didn't have to fight like we did. But so many of them still do . . .*

"She's brave enough," volunteered one of Hannah's university colleagues. "I mean, hey, I'm closeted. I can't be out; in my department they'd make my life a living hell and find a way to fire me. Hannah stands up to the dean, the provost, everyone. She assigns her students the complete works of Lillian Fader-man. She takes them to poetry slams!" *Yes*, thought Hannah, *but I don't think my relatives who fled Poland would see standing in front of a lectern as an act of valor.*

55

"Can you give it a rest?" begged Zoe. "I mean, school is out. This is party time. Pass the beer, please." She snapped the cap off with her sharp white teeth and raised the bottle high. "I'll say it. Here's to women warriors!"

"To women warriors," they all said, but Tina poured some liquor on the ground, murmuring *ancestors*.

After a dinner of barbecued chicken and veggie kabobs, they set up the annual volleyball game. A drunken match began, with bumps and spikes directed everywhere but over the net. Cries of "Watch it!," "Ow!," and "You moron!" resounded between shrieks of laughter. Yet another misdirected shot sent the abused volleyball rolling into the bushes. "I'll get it," yelled Hannah, who had returned to the campfire pit and was trying (and failing) to muster spiritual preparation for the sweat lodge. She kicked off her Birkenstocks, enjoying the coolness of soft lawn underfoot, and ambled after the lost game ball.

What was bravery? She couldn't decide. Her own wartime heroines were peace activists: Jeannette Rankin, the first woman ever elected to Congress, a pacifist suffragist who had dared to vote against America's entry into World War I. On April 7, 1917, she had declared in the Roll Call of the U.S. House of Representatives, "I want to stand by my country—but I cannot vote for war. I vote NO." And Hannah's lectures typically valorized nurses and healers who transcended barriers of hate—like Susan King Taylor, the African American nurse and former slave who served with the 33rd U.S. Colored Troops during the Civil War, teaching Union soldiers to write—whether they were black or white.

She had never been in a war herself. Hannah had spent part of her 1960s childhood marching for peace, head-banded, earnest, skipping one day in third grade to hold a poster at a vigil with her mom. Then the Vietnam War had ended—or imploded—and America returned to its Cold War against the Evil Empire, the same Russians who had been allies in both

World Wars. The 1980s had directed American anxiety to the possibility of nuclear war. But in the streets a different war was raging, too: AIDS and hate crimes, crack addiction, rape. Nearly every one of Hannah's friends had survived rape or hate violence.

Well, in her twenties she had certainly fought on all those fronts, in those culture wars. Writing, speaking, marching, she had fought alongside dying men, whose wracked bodies filled the unseen trenches of ignorance and fear and rejection. She had marched in every Take Back the Night rally alongside girlfriends too brutalized to receive the gentlest touch in bed from a woman's hand.

And what counted as bravery in the long war against homophobia? She remembered a night at a different women's bar, in a tough city neighborhood somewhere in the Midwest, where she had a summer teaching appointment. She was dancing with a friend, but left early, alone, only to find her parked car covered, hood to tail light, with local gang members. They knew where she had been. They called to her, not moving off her car as she walked up with keys in hand. *You gay?* they taunted, knowing. *You a dyke?*

"Yes, I am! What would you like to know?" she'd cheerfully sassed back, as if this were a sex ed class and not a confrontation. But even under pressure, Hannah was most comfortably empowered as a scholar. She stood there as if in class. *I have the answers to your questions. Raise your hand.* They weren't expecting this. They scrambled, fled, apologizing, sheepish.

"Ow!" Hannah felt a stinging sharpness in her right heel. Almost tripping over a log, she steadied herself against the nearest tree and bent over to see what she had stepped on. It was a porcupine quill, the barb almost but not quite penetrating her spring-tender foot. Great. Now she would have rabies. Hurling the volleyball back in the direction of her barmates, Hannah sat down on a log with a grunt of pain, rocking her foot and trying to remember first-aid approaches to a puncture wound.

"*Nyet.* I do," said a voice. Confused, Hannah stood up. There was no one there.

"Sit. I do," the voice said again, and it was the founder of the Women's Battalion of Death, the great Russian warrior Maria Bochkareva, who now filled the space of the growing spring dusk with her muddied, sweat-stained bulk. Without waiting for invitation, she bent down and yanked the quill out of Hannah's foot.

"OW!" gasped Hannah. "Who the—what do you think you're *doing?*" For a panicked minute she thought the woman might be a lost deer hunter, but it was the wrong season. It was spring. Wasn't it? Hannah looked back frantically in the direction of the volleyball party, but there was no longer any sign of the campfire, the cabin, or her rowdy lesbian friends. The sky had darkened to crisp autumn hues. The trees around them were shedding leaves; the leaves that hit the ground rapidly silvered with veins of frost crystals; the earth beneath her other bare foot had frozen and hardened. In the distance, she heard explosions.

Maria uncorked a flask concealed beneath her tunic. "No problem, *wodka,*" she explained, and then held out her dirty, trailing sleeve. "You bite." When Hannah did not move, the woman sighed and pointed to a clean spot on the soiled wool. "My arm, you bite it, NOW," she commanded. Hannah lifted the flesh of the stranger's well-built forearm to her lips just as Bochkareva bent and splashed a stinging shot of vodka into Hannah's open wound.

"OY!" Now Hannah readily clamped onto Maria's arm. "SHIT, that hurt."

"The foot, ha, is nothing," sneered Maria, recapped the flask and flopping down beside Hannah on the now-rotten log. "You want howl, you want ugly, you want die, you have belly wound. You have lung wound. You pull icicle out of *eye,* like my Elena, and keep shooting." She quickly turned and flung herself below the log, flat, motionless, as a fox scampered through a pile of twigs beyond them. "Get down, idiot city girl. Get head down, rifle up!"

"I don't have a rifle! I'm . . . this is just a campout, a party," Hannah ventured. "This isn't a war. Get that rifle away from me! Who are you shooting at?"

"Kaiser men," whispered Maria. Her neck bulged with veins as she strained to listen, her head cocked to one side. But around that neck was a cord entwining religious medals and a tiny gray fabric bag. *So, it's true,* Hannah marveled, having read that all of the women enlisted in Bochkareva's Battalion of Death carried suicide poison in a pouch close to their throats. Rather than be captured alive and endure the dishonor of rape, they would defy their assailants and choose the very hour of their deaths, exiting unviolated. That poison capsule must have nestled uneasily against the sacred cross on the same necklace: suicide, a mortal sin. The Mother Church was supposed to decide who and when to martyr, female agency in such matters rarely recognized. Yet Bochkareva had been addressed as "Mister Commander"; had written, of her own battle experience, "We were eager to get into the fray to show the Germans what we, the boys of the Fifth Regiment, could do. Were we nervous? Undoubtedly. But it was not the nervousness of cowardice. . . . our hands were steady." Although she had been ready to kill, the Russian woman's own memoir had emphasized the saving of lives.

It gave me immense joy to sustain life in benumbed human bodies. As I was kneeling over one such wounded, who had suffered a great loss of blood, and was about to lift him, a sniper's bullet hit me between the thumb and forefinger and passed on and through the flesh of my left forearm. . . . I continued my work all night, and was recommended "for bravery in defensive and offensive fighting and for rendering, while wounded, first aid on the field of battle," to receive the Cross of St. George. But I never received it. Instead, I was awarded a medal of the 4th degree and was informed that a woman could not obtain the Cross of St. George. . . . I protested to the Commander.

Now the great Bochkareva pulled Hannah up and hustled both of them further into the woods. Twigs snapped and cracked below Hannah's throbbing heel, forcing her to give up thoughts about Russian sexism and move as directed by the powerful figure. In another moment, both of them spotted the looming shape of Janey and Amy's tree fort.

It had, indeed, become a fort. The gauzy print blankets and pillows Janey and Amy had set up just that morning, for the comfort of potential midnight couples seeking a love nest, were nowhere to be seen. Crouched on the deck, clad in parachute harness with only a missing tooth to mar her beauty, was the Nazi fighter Hannah had been named for, the Hungarian Jewish martyr Hannah Senesh.

"Got good one for you. You train her!" Maria called up. "Only tiny wound. In *heel*, like Achilles. Make her tough, my sister! I go." With a rough pat on Hannah's back, she turned and disappeared into the woods. And the 22-year-old warrior standing ready in the tree fort gazed down at her namesake and growled, "Get up here before they see you, *girlchik.*"

No. No.

Not this. Not Nazi Germany.

No way.

I've got to get out of this one. I can't do this one. I don't want to know.

I'll die if I go up into that tree with her. They're coming for her. They tortured her. They killed her!

"Yes, I know. You lecture on war from the safety of a class-room," Senesh taunted, peeling off her parachute and laying it aside. "You want some women's history? 'Life hangs over me like a question mark. I could have been twenty-three next July; I gambled on what mattered most. The dice were cast. I lost.' Can you be brave, Hannah? They quote my poetry, so often, but that is not all I wrote. I once wrote, on Christmas night of 1943 while I trained as a partisan, 'I respect the people who believe in something, respect their idealistic struggle with the daily realities. I respect those who don't live just for the moment, or for money. . . . We have need of one thing: people who are brave and without prejudices—who want to think for themselves and not accept outmoded ideas.' " She smiled fiercely. "You think I don't know that it takes guts to be a lesbian scholar, to get up every day and face the students and be out? They would have killed you, here. So, run. *Run*. Don't let your tender heel slow you down; don't pause before doing the right thing. Stay brave in your war." And she ducked, as booted footsteps crashed toward them, too close, and coming nearer.

Hannah stumbled, gasping, back toward the campfire, the party. Would anyone have noticed her absence? What time was it? What season? Bochkareva had vanished. The frost that had appeared on mulch underfoot was now giving way to tender green shoots. Hannah looked back over her shoulder and saw, deep within the woods, a plume of smoke rising, dissipating instantly as it touched sky.

As she emerged from the woods, it was once again warm spring; but now it was Saturday morning, not the previous evening, and Shoni and Meg were at the entrance to the sweat lodge, calling to her. "Hurry up. Where have you been? The stones are hot. It's time."

If I can just sit down, thought Hannah, and *think*. If I can just take some time to sit, to sit here in community, maybe I'll sort it out. I have my own past. I don't know why I'm being placed in everyone else's story. Maybe I'm supposed to meditate on bravery. What am I being prepared for? Are these women telling me to get ready to be a warrior? *I don't know if that's what I am supposed to do.* But she entered the lodge.

Silent heat. Burning stones.

In the sweat lodge, reduced to naked vulnerability, Hannah and her friends opened to the messages of their very different ancestors. Traditions met, melted, and pooled around their feet. Their hot bodies steamed as Shoni led them through the ritual of greeting their many martyred peoples, their spiritual leaders. As each woman welcomed in her own past, it seemed they could feel the presence of those watchful visitors. Much later in the day, when it was all over, Hannah would overhear Shoni say to Isabel, "That was one crowded lodge."

As her increasingly drenched body shifted and turned on one dark patch of earth, Hannah's mind turned over that question of bravery, of survival in wartime. Who had been brave? Her immigrant foremothers, crossing the Atlantic, destitute, driven, fleeing pogroms. Because they left Europe when they had, few in her own family had faced Hitler. She knew there had been hardship, arrests, the long voyage in a ship. Were they warriors? Victims? Survivors? Or all of that and colonizers, too, moving with their fragile menorah candelabras into tenements built on Mohawk lands?

It was too hot. There wasn't enough air. She was holding earth in her fists but around her was the angry ocean, America so far away it was just an idea. She sensed the other women around her locked in their own visions of ancestors, who had come unwillingly in slave ships or as indentured servants or sex trafficked as whores. All of them except Shoni and Meg had lineage that came from somewhere else. All of them, including Shoni and Meg, descended from those who had suffered far more in wartime, slavery, genocide, the Trail of Tears, internment camps, mental institutions for the queers.

Their sweat was gone. Their skins were baking. Meg, knowing the uninitiated were struggling in the intense dry heat, abruptly dashed ladles of water across their bodies. And in an instant Hannah was standing at the rails of an immigrant ship. The slap of water was refreshing, but was salt: a wave of dense seawater, drowning her. It drenched her scarf. Her head was covered, modestly. She held a baby. Both of them cried out.

Now she couldn't breathe. The air felt both absent and too close. Her head was pounding, her body shaking. Around her she sensed her other friends, too, were wrestling with visions and visitations not altogether easy to contain in their damp bodies. For the moment, though, there was only her own need to escape, to get out. She couldn't stop to take in Gloria's moaning or Nan's

repeated mumbling of "I see you; I know you; I can hear you."
They were all packed together. Too many of them.

They were all packed together because they were on their way
to Auschwitz.

The sweat lodge was a boxcar.

I bear the burden of my own genetic code.

The train would carry her into her ancestry, but she might
never come back. Why was she so unable to face that fear? How
could she be her own ancestors' spiritual descendent if she lacked
bravery?

*Open the door. Raise the sides. Make a window. More and more
ancestors are flying in. There's no more room. Their haunting can't
protect me. We need to get out of here.* "I need to get out of here,"
Hannah hissed. Meg, calm and concerned simultaneously, ladled
water onto Hannah's head, but the images hovered nonetheless.
The wrapped walls still held the shape and splintered finality of
a boxcar. Then Shoni called out "Ho!" and opened the draped
entrance to the lodge. There was a collective exaltation of anguish
and relief. Several women dropped their heads to their dirt-caked
knees and wept, but Hannah rose from the soft dirt floor and
lurched on wobbly legs through the entrance, which was finally
an exit from the lodge as well.

Immediately, she could breathe again, although cold sweat
began to mat her already wet hair. The day was beautiful. There
wasn't a hint of disturbance in the circle of trees around the quiet
lodge, and women's laughter poured out of the house where
everyone else was gathering to make lunch. *Isabel.* She had to talk
to Isabel. With more purpose in her stride than she had ever
summoned before, Hannah burst into the house, dripping,
muddied, naked but for her pine needle-plastered underpants,
shouting *"Isabel! Isabel!"*

Her friend, their bartender, was in the kitchen mixing fresh
lemonade with spring flowers, using a pair of silver tongs. She
looked up, surprised. And then, grabbing a dishtowel, wrapped
it around Hannah's shoulders and pulled her into the cabin's rustic bathroom, calling "Just give us a moment" over one shoulder

to the other gaping party guests. Isabel latched the bathroom door and poured water from the faucet into a plastic Wonder Woman cup left on the sink. Patting Hannah's arm, she ordered, "Drink this, but swallow slowly."

Hannah ignored the directive and gulped. Then retched. "This is just water, right?" she demanded angrily. "It's not one of your *drinks?*" Isabel shook her head, watchful and silent now.

They sat together on the curved rim of Janey and Amy's old-fashioned bathtub, which was fortunately broad enough and stable underneath them. Hannah waited until her heartbeat had slowed down to something approximating normal, and finally faced her friend. "Listen, Isabel." She spoke with all the authority, all the practiced firmness of her most empowered classroom voice, the one she used to warn her students that plagiarism and cheating could not be tolerated. "I don't know what's happening to me lately. I don't know how much you have to do with it, or even if it's you. And I don't know if these little *encounters* are something you think I asked for or that I need. Because I never see them coming, and mostly they're okay. But don't send me into the Holocaust. Are we clear on that point? Don't send me there. I can't learn anything new there. I'm busy living for all of them; I'm not supposed to endure what they did all over again." She blew her nose on a wad of toilet paper and was startled to see blood. "I'm not brave like Hannah Senesh. I'm not ready to be a martyr, even in a vision." She gasped as she caught sight of her reflection in the mirror: for a moment, it appeared that all the hair had been shorn from her head. She grabbed at Isabel, and they toppled over into the bathtub.

"Don't make me feel pain," Hannah begged. Then she noticed the candle. There was a candle burning in a dish on the bathroom windowsill, a beeswax memorial candle in a protective glass jar.

"I put that there for Memorial Day," said Isabel, and as she pushed up the window to let in more air, the breeze of spring blew out the candle flame. "For your warrior ancestor Hannah Senesh. Let's quote her, and then you'll feel better, all right.

'Blessed is the match, consumed in kindling flame,'" recited Isabel; abruptly, Hannah went limp.

When she woke up, one hour later, Hannah found she had been washed clean and dressed in a white bathrobe. Her hair, now drying, fell fully from her cooled brow. She was in the cabin's spacious and beautifully sunlit living room, with the other members of the campout who had participated in the sweat lodge, all in terrycloth robes, some also with awed looks or tears drying on their faces. Ritually prepared foods were passed around, and Hannah accepted a bowl of potatoes. They ate in silence. Then Moira said, "There was a time for my people when one-quarter of one potato meant the difference between living and dying."

"And mine," said Hannah.

"And mine," said Letty. And as Hannah waited to see who might speak next, her eyes fell on the chess table in the corner, and for an instant she saw Rose Valland, the librarian, playing with Jeanette Rankin, the Congresswoman, each attempting to win a game of strategy without enacting violence. "Well, it's your move," Rankin was saying.

"Check," answered Valland, with a barely discernable smirk. Then no one was there. The chairs were empty. And while the rest of that weekend held its usual pleasures, from skinny-dipping in the creek to late-night marshmallow roasts, Hannah turned her head and carefully looked away from the rising campfire smoke, which bent eastward; and Isabel put away the game of chess some guests had started and abandoned. An unseen hand had knocked the queen far over, on her edge.

Chapter Six
Pride Week

"What was your first Pride Parade like?"

Awkwardly bent over the front bumper of her students' LGBT Association parade float, Hannah was so surprised by the question that she dropped her wrench. It made a loud clang on the garage floor of the campus physical plant shed, and the other students all looked up, startled. Rainbow-themed crepe paper and a half-inked banner declaring *Intersectionality Is Our Strength* trailed from their stained hands.

There was nothing more stupefying than being reminded that she, their professor of LGBT history, was some kind of historical artifact herself.

"Well." Hannah sat down on the hood of the Chevette and tried to remember. "I was like you, or some of you, just finishing up my first year of college. Newly out, terrified, broke. I didn't really hang out in bars, so a Pride parade was something free and open that I could watch without much investment, and of course there were women to check out . . ." She caught herself, wondering how much to reveal to rising sophomores.

They could have cared less about student-teacher boundaries; school was out for summer. "I bet you were a stone fox," breathed Emma, who had spent all spring angling to be teacher's pet.

"I was not a stone butch, that's for sure," Hannah laughed.

"You can draw the picture yourself, can't you? What do you think I looked like at Pride '79?"

"Overalls, Birkenstocks, plaid flannel shirt," they shouted in chorus.

"Yes, and the requisite purple bandanna. I did have punk friends, but piercings and tattoos became more of a common look later on."

"Do you have a tattoo now?" Emma wanted to know. "Where is it?" Her eyes darted across Hannah's body, and Hannah silently thanked the Goddess for the over-21 rule at Sappho's Bar and Grill, where she'd be partying with her own peers after tomorrow's parade.

"Yes, Emma, I have a tattoo," she heard herself sharing, and rolled up her pants leg to reveal the rippling Greek letters along her right calf muscle. The students examined her body art, puzzled. "That looks like an Alpha and a Phi. You were in a sorority?" asked Caitlin, confused. "You don't seem the type."

"Moron! It's the name of Sappho," Emma shot back.

"Back to my first Pride parade, if you please. Well, I was living at home that June, and it was Father's Day weekend, you know, as Pride so often falls on, and I was supposed to do something nice with my dad. We were quite close. He promised to teach me to ride a motorcycle that day, and oh, how I looked forward to that, but at the same time I was itching to sneak away to the parade I knew was being held downtown. Somehow, I worked up the nerve to come out to him while we were riding around the countryside. He said he didn't mind having a daughter who was a Dyke on a Bike as long as I always wore a helmet. Then he actually dropped me off at the head of the parade as if I were going to be the lead bike. I was mortified, but what a cool spirit he was! And I spent the rest of that afternoon watching women, but shaking with adrenaline that I had just come out to my father, and he didn't mind. In fact, he was proud of me ..."

Dad. Dad. Dad.

She went home pleased with her students' parade float, but missing her father. Too many of those students had shared the

68

pain of being rejected by their families. Coming out in a homo-phobic home had meant, for some of them, a father's contempt expressed in blows and curses. But Hannah, twice their age, had been blessed with loving parents, light years ahead on the toler-ance curve. Her father had been that rare guy who wrote out Christmas checks for lesbian separatist organizations and partied with dyke celebrities, rolling them joints. Though Hannah had spent decades chanting *death to the patriarchy*, her arms linked with separatist pals, she owed her chops in activism and service to her dad, and she still followed many progressive causes he embraced in the 1960s. His devoted stewardship for Mother Earth practically guaranteed that she would end up spending her adult summers living in an owl-haunted pup tent backstage at women's music festivals, doing recycling. During his stint as a stay-at-home father while finishing his own graduate thesis, he had written feisty letters to Hannah's third-grade teacher, defending her right to wear pants to school instead of a dress. He had not really intended to raise a little lesbian, but once Han-nah came out as a gay eighteen-year-old, he stepped up to the plate with harsh words for parents who dissed or abandoned their gay children. *That*, to him, was heresy. And now he was gone.

What had she done after that first Gay Pride event? Too bash-ful to linger and flirt, she had ducked into the local women's bookstore, Amazons and Pages, and promptly fallen in love with women's history. Those shelves of radical first editions, some of them signed! Women who were gay in the seventeenth century! She ended up getting a part-time summer job in the bookshop. Soon she was making out in the stacks with the co-manager, their bandannas and Birkenstocks cast off and co-mingling on the cocoa-brown carpet of the Women's History aisle.

But the more Hannah read and researched, the more her les-bian pride came with a side dish of shame, and it sure wasn't about the sex act itself. How was she supposed to deal with these newly discovered lesbian foremothers who, apparently, were racist and classist Jew-phobic jerks?

69

It had shocked her. Earlier, in high school, she'd naively assumed that any woman in the oppressive Olden Days who gained access to power would surely help empower other women. Then she learned how Queen Isabella expelled both Jews and Muslims from Spain, how white Southern women whose husbands secretly raped their slaves then had those slave women punished further still. Elizabeth Cady Stanton mocked Irish and Catholic immigrants, thus alienating many Irish women immigrants who might have joined the suffrage movement. The great filmmaker Leni Riefenstahl made propaganda films for Adolf Hitler; Oveta Culp Hobby, who directed the first Women's Army Corps, wouldn't integrate the troops; nor were talented black women welcome in the All-American Girls Baseball League. Japanese-American women desperately hoping to get out of World War II internment camps in the Western states were rejected by Seven Sisters colleges. Margaret Sanger's early birth control movement was full of bold feminists—including women who supported sterilizing the "unfit."

Now, at 19, she was discovering that lesbians, too, came with as many prejudices as straight folks. The writer Patricia Highsmith obsessively disliked Jews. Natalie Barney, who held so many visionary lesbian salons in Paris, had a pro-Fascist, anti-Semitic streak too; her very beautiful lover, artist Romaine Brooks, jeered Gertrude Stein as "an uneducated Jew." Even Gertrude Stein herself, a Jew in love with a Jew—Alice B. Toklas—ignored the Holocaust. And what about P.L. Travers, the probably lesbian author of all those Mary Poppins books? Her tales were riddled with black stereotypes. And Radclyffe Hall? Judging herself tasteful in never depicting all-out sex scenes, living in the rarefied air of the upper class, she identified with "the worthy among the inverted . . . those fine men and women whom Nature has seen fit to set apart as variants." And then there was that lesbian who infiltrated other lesbians' meetings as an anti-Communist informer for the FBI, and . . .

No one was perfect. No one loved everyone. One could still take pride in what lesbians, as a group, had accomplished in the face of unrelenting hostility across every culture. But how could she rationalize being attracted to so many of the individual women in history who were so flawed? Even scarier, what were her own biases?

Immersed in women's history, she found plenty of lesbian pride. But like others, Hannah had hoped to find a unifying, divine love in the community she was claiming.

This year Hannah began her Pride Day at Sappho's, spending the morning on a volunteer crew decorating for the big after-party. Isabel had provided the work team with a delicious brunch: little quiches, salmon and cream cheese and bagels, platters of hummus and sliced tomatoes, very dark and rich coffee. Hannah remained quiet and thoughtful as she looped lavender daisies around ceiling beams and barstools. Finally she burst out: "When we came out, Pride was a big deal, right? It was a statement to be seen there. How do I deal with some of my students who just don't care about Pride, or the women who came before them? They're not political at all. You know, when I first came out, I identified as a lesbian even before I had actually had sex. Now I have female students who are having sex with one another without ever identifying as lesbians. It's like they skipped a step."

"Aw, straight girls who experiment always fell into that category," Carol shrugged.

"It's false consciousness," growled Yvette.

"My first Pride? It was Pride for guys, not us dykes. I was 86'd from the men's bar because I was a *woman*," Letty huffed.

Isabel, who seldom entered debates such as these, spoke up unexpectedly. "Hannah, you always expect your students to care as much as you do about 'famous' lesbians from the twentieth century and earlier. Their role models may be ordinary women, lesbians and gay men they know personally. Besides," she added with a grin, "remember that joke that everyone thinks they were someone 'famous' in a past life? Why don't we honor ordinary women, at Pride?"

"Or year round?" agreed Yvette.

"I know. It's like every year at Pride we hear about what was done TO homos or done FOR us by well-meaning straight people who passed civil rights ordinances." Tina waved her roll of crepe paper as if it were a cutlass. "What about what we did ourselves, just in terms of—you know—daily survival?"

"Well, what's ordinary pride, then? I mean, what do we admire in ordinary lesbians?" Hannah asked. "You tell me." She sat back on her heels, glad for a break from hanging streamers, and took a bite of quiche, which melted in her mouth.

Nobody spoke for a moment. Isabel, hiding a small smile behind a coffee mug, turned back to tidying the bar. Then Letty said, "We always had the highest regard here for dykes who had skills we could use. Didn't matter if they were rich, educated, famous, published, or glamour-puss beautiful. It was, Hi, can you get these newsletters mimeographed for free in your office at work without being caught? Can you get the best deal for the softball uniforms? Can you hammer, do lights for dances, rewire a stereo?"

"And butch skills, basic butch pride," Yvette suggested. "Taking pride in knowing how to tie a tie right, change your own oil, build a ramp."

"What about femme skills?" Carol shot back. "I was the first one here to choose to be a lesbian mom. Had my daughter through artificial insemination, so I kept my gold star lez card. I became a mother, but I never had sex with a man."

"You could *afford* to buy frozen sperm," Letty argued. "My ma never married. You all know I'm the daughter of a rape. My sheroes are everyday women *survivors.*"

"My lesbian P.E. teacher risked her job by coaching me after school."

"My lesbian aunt took me to the movies every Sunday because we didn't have a TV. She saved her money to treat me when she never went out herself."

"Pride is getting sober." "Pride is taking your abuser to court." "Pride is getting undressed in the locker room at the gym after you've lost a breast to cancer." Hannah, on her heels, marveling at their endless lists, the extraordinary in the ordinary.

Finally, Carol, who worked at the bureau of social services, gave Hannah a friendly swat. "Your kids will get political as soon as they start looking for jobs and find out it's still a man's world. Come on, let's go check out the parade. Didn't some of your students make a float? Let's go support them."

At the parade, nursing a Creamsicle, Hannah stood on the curb, incognito and uncomfortable as hot men in black leather thongs danced on floating fantasy themes pulled by dog-collared "slave" youths. She tried to remain nonjudgmental for two minutes. Yes, her students had a float; here it came. And yes, she was proud of them. Their signs celebrated the LGBT minor she'd help establish at the university. These were future historians and scholars. They waved at her, looking joyful, alive, young.

She watched as her students' float rolled away, followed by a tough-looking lesbian crew. "Whoa! Look at *that* brigade," marveled Hannah, poking Carol to get her attention. If Pride Day had become unalterably commercialized in recent years, brands and bank logos and rainbow vodka ads flapping from every awning and banner, at least this flotilla of dykes declared *old school*. Led by one battered motorcycle, the women walked four abreast, an army of amazons. She stood on the curb transfixed.

"Where?" Carol frowned. "I don't see anything."

"What do you mean? They're right in front of us," Hannah insisted, and then both her own blood temperature and that of the mild June air seemed to plunge twenty or thirty degrees as she realized what she was seeing.

It was a ghost crew. Where a woman's bicep tightened, where a foot picked up to march a step ahead, there were wavy parentheses like the shedding of dust, and Hannah could see right through the boots and leather jacket sleeves for an instant before the formation of women solidified again. Together, they shimmered, then solidified, shimmered, growing transparent and fading, then colorful again. Hannah now saw that the marching feet did not disturb the litter in the street, that the brightly packaged condoms and tossed candies left by each preceding Pride contingent did not stick to the soles of the shoes walking along now. The flag they held did not move in the wind. It had, she now saw, only forty-eight stars. These were dykes of the 1930s, '40s, '50s.

They had small signs around their necks. *I am Lorraine Hansberry. I am Louise Fitzhugh. I am Lisa Ben. I am Natalie Barney.* They were writers! On a small float they pulled along, two women sat cross-legged at a makeshift desk, reaching by turns into apple crates piled high with books. They flung the books at Hannah: bad pulp novels about doomed lesbian affairs, classic paperbacks with actual lesbian authors—she knew them all. These were the signed first editions she had discovered at her first women's bookstore after her first Pride parade in 1979, the difficult, flawed authors she had nonetheless chosen to love. As the books landed at her feet, each flopped open to the signed frontispiece page ever so briefly, and then vanished in a spray of lavender smoke.

"God damn it! Are you sure you're not seeing this?" Hannah pulled frantically at Carol's arm. But Carol was pointing to the next float, already approaching: "Look, Hannah, there's our mayor. She finally came to Pride."

She needed a drink. Sappho's would be packed by now, of course: It was Pride Day. There were six or more men's bars in the community, but only one exclusively for women, and after hours of being jostled by semi-clad males intent on cruising, quite a few lesbian activists would be ready to dive into a cool martini at the bar—before, perhaps, diving into one another. A celebration in womanspace. Pride in what all of them had created, there in that valley: community.

Hannah dropped Carol at her house, saying nothing more about the ghost crew she was certain she'd seen at the parade, and then headed over to Sappho's parking lot. Motorcycles filled more than half the spaces. She could hear bellowed laughter, the ring of the cash register, and oldies music: an inviting vibe. Making sure she had her wallet and camera for the occasion, Hannah pushed open the door to the bar.

The first thing she noticed was the coat rack. In summer Isabel kept the coat rack in the back storeroom, or the Nook, since no one came in with the bulky outer layers of winter months. Hannah herself was clad just in shorts and an old Olivia Records T-shirt. But the coat rack was now fully assembled in the entry hall, and on its pegs she saw an expansion of thick black jackets. Leather jackets of the old-school variety: the jackets of the parade crew.

And at the bar, belting down shots, were Louise Fitzhugh, Barbara Gittings, Lorraine Hansberry, Barbara Grier, Lisa Ben, Patricia Highsmith, more figures she could not yet identify, a line of lesbian authors and playwrights and editors who had risen out of the McCarthy era and published the paper trail of literary pride, identity, creative life, the honor of the daring written word.

Isabel was pouring them drinks from two tumblers marked BUTCH and FEMME.

Every woman at the bar turned and looked at Hannah, who stood slack-jawed in the doorway; but there was no screech of barstool as these bodies turned; for ghosts don't make old metal grind. And yet they called to her. "What'll it be, missy?" shouted one.

"I told you, no talking, Highsmith! Just because I read you doesn't mean that I won't toss you out," Isabel warned, acting as both barmaid and bouncer as if everything were terribly routine. And Barbara Grier, the irascible founder of Naiad Books, leaned past Isabel and told Patricia Highsmith, "That last manuscript of yours? If Jesus Christ crawled on his knees, he couldn't get that thing published."

Then Hannah realized that while she could see the ghost brigade of lesbian pioneers, and so, it seemed, could Isabel, there were in fact two other living women from their own era at the bar. The two oldest regulars, who had patronized the bar before it became Sappho's, were drinking too. Could they see the "visitors" amongst them? Isabel busily served one and all with the same ebullient professionalism she brought to any occasion, as if this were not a Pride party for the dead. Amid the shimmering ghost writers, the stoic elder tomboy they all called Trale (and sometimes more affectionately Trale Blazer) was sipping cognac at the bar. And Letty was now sprawled in the armchair by the chessboard, tipping up a beer and reading *People,* clearly not interested in the classic lesbian fiction written by the literary figures now floating around her.

"Hello, Doc," said Trale, nodding to Hannah and patting the barstool beside her. "Think this one's empty. Getting rather crowded in here, huh?" Her long eyes twinkled.

"So you see them too," Hannah ventured, in complete wonderment. *It must be in the drinks! But I haven't even had one yet.* She watched as Trale nodded and sipped.

"What do you think's really going on?" Hannah dared ask her. "I mean, if you don't mind my asking. If you see what I see."

"Well, I don't have much to say," said Trale. "I was in here tuning the piano when they all came in. I have opinions. But I keep them to myself. You're the history teacher. Isn't your business past lives?" She pushed a small glass toward Hannah. "Why don't you try this? It's called a Wooden Floor. A favorite of us carpenters from the 1970s, but careful. It'll make you want to lie down."

Hoping to impress Trale, Hannah threw back the shot, noticing telltale signs of Isabel's herbal mixture in the foam left on the glass. What would happen next? "I can see these women all around you. I know who they are. You know, for Pride Week I just set up a display at the library honoring these earlier lesbians who made the culture happen. But I never expected to encounter their ghosts at the parade, or at the bar!" She could feel leather jackets stirring on their pegs, as if demanding a place in the conversation. She could feel the drink heating up her legs and arms.

"You encounter me at the bar pretty often," said Trale. "And I'm an earlier lesbian. By the way, I'm not a ghost. Not saying you should honor me, just that you can ask me questions about the past if you're inclined. Can't always ask the dead, though on some nights they just won't shut up, huh?"

Hannah digested this. "I'm sorry, Trale. I guess I've never really taken the time to sit down and talk to you, have I?"

"Well, you know, it's like the *Wizard of Oz*. I watch you go chasing all over for lesbian history, and there's plenty of it right here in your own backyard," Trale pointed out, with a sideways look. "I was in this bar before Isabel bought it. Here's the thing: I could tell you stories. I'm older than I look." She took out a cracked leather wallet from her hip pocket and pushed out her driver's license with a calloused thumb.

Hannah gasped at the date. "You're not THAT old!"

"Maintenance," said Trale, patting her slim hips. "Athlete, vegetarian. Just some cognac at the weekend—or during Pride," and she gestured to Isabel with her glass.

Hannah felt the courage to ask questions unfurling in her muscles like a banner. "Trale, do *you* sometimes meet up with past lives, here?"

"Just on special occasions," said eighty-six-year-old Trale, who looked no more than sixty, and she reached out to grab the floating waist of Natalie Barney, who paused and smooched a kiss on Trale's cheekbone. "She was a good kisser, in her day. You think she didn't try to make me, too? Jesus . . . she had every woman. Paris salons, full of artists. Too rich for my blood! I was just a studio musician for the military band."

"You were in Europe? You actually knew these lesbians?"

"I was there briefly with the army. I stayed and helped rebuild some of their houses as they aged; sort of a chore-boy to the ritzy, you might say. It's kind of a blur now. I saved some of their writings from being pitched out or stolen when they died," and Trale raised her glass in tribute to the ghost-dyke lives around them. Ghosts raised their drinks in turn. "Remember that the hired hands always know what's going on in the lives of the famous. I varnished their window sills, put in fencing; I heard their conversations. Just outlived 'em, that's all. I'm open to seeing past lives; it's not the drink. Although the booze here has its special charms," and she leaned over the bar and squeezed Isabel, who turned and chided, "*Trale.*"

"How did you deal with the downside of these women—their racism, their Jew-baiting, their dysfunctional love affairs?"

"You act like you're naïve," said Trale. "You know all that is still part of the culture now. Maybe better hidden."

"Well, what was the old bar like?" Hannah asked. "I mean, before Isabel bought it."

"Ah." Trale looked up at the ceiling affectionately. "Well, as you know, it was called the Overhead, partly because it cost so much to keep it going and none of us had any money, and then we were all in over our heads volunteering here at a time when you could get queerbashed going to a known dyke bar. It was a good time and a not-good time. Don't idealize the old days. There were bar fights and, yeah, there was racism, and of course a lot of smoking, a lot of alcoholism. Some women came in pretty damaged. We had anger that we used as best we could. We were always trying to harness people's energy. One night I was really angry and wanted to hit something. Right away Letty said, Come over here; we need this wall down. It was down in ten minutes." She smiled, reminiscing. "We had a period of time when the actual wood bar wasn't finished. Sue broke her wrist, then never got around to putting a hinge on the unfinished section, so when you leaned on it just right, drinks went flying. Anyway, one night Letty emphasized her point with her fist. Her beer flew straight up, she caught it with her left hand, and never missed a beat."

She paused. "We did think we were doing something special. We did make a time capsule." She looked up at the ceiling again as if remembering. Then Trale closed her long eyes, and Hannah watched the flick beneath the lids that spoke Trale's thoughts.

A time capsule! Hannah remembered imagining how cool that would be, musing over what it might contain. When had she thought of that? Wasn't it just three months ago, on the night of the Passover Seder? She tapped Trale's arm. "What's in it? Is it still here?"

"Oh, you know. Old-school stuff. Bottle of apricot brandy, photos of some New Year's Eve revues, a Sisterhood Is Powerful tank top, a wrench, one dyke's dishonorable discharge papers from the Air Force, that Lesbian Concentrate album, some poems, a softball glove. I won't tell you where it is. Isabel knows, though."

She keeps looking up at the ceiling. I bet it's in the disco ball. No one would ever think to look there and no one would take it down. It's in the disco ball! It's the pride in ordinary lives, just like everyone was saying this morning. Look at Trale; she lived through decade after decade, on the outskirts of the famous, an ordinary dyke. But she's the one who's here and who remembers. She's the pride keeper here, the ordinary hero, good at everything she does. Good at whatever everyone needs. And I've been so busy chasing the rude, famous foremothers I've never had a drink with Trale.

"I was there at Stonewall, too," added Trale. "And then at Woodstock. There in the background at all of it. Because I built some stages and tuned pianos."

"Trale Blazer," marveled Hannah. "Can I ask you for a dance?"

"I think you already have," said Trale, but Hannah would not understand what she meant for many more months, and Trale took pity on her now. "Of course you want to dance now; you just drank a Wooden Floor. Okay. But I lead."

The ghosts gathered around them. That was when the bar's very old piano, the one Trale had tuned earlier that day, began playing "Smoke Gets In Your Eyes," although no one—no woman that Hannah could see—was seated on the bench to touch the keys.

Chapter Seven
The Fourth of July

High summer, and the fireflies blinked Morse Code to Hannah as she rested and recovered and researched and wrote. Could there be a better life than this, rising lazily to brew her Hawaiian coffee, playing her women's music compilations, sketching chapter outlines for her next women's history book, until the bicycle in the hallway called her to get up and explore her favorite trail? The rain held off. The heat lightning patterns at dusk were dazzling, not threatening. The tomatoes grew, snugly promising bursts of juiciness. Evenings at Sappho's ranged from pinochle to board games to movies and softball.

There was just one factor keeping the upcoming holiday weekend from being pretty damn serene. Regrettably, the notorious right-wing "Take Back Our United States" conference and rally was once again scheduled for Fourth of July, and Hannah ground her teeth daily as their posters, flyers, and bumper stickers began appearing all over town. *HOMOSEXUALS CAN CHANGE*, one slogan assured. Less kindly was the ubiquitous broadside *TAKE BACK OUR UNITED STATES! FIGHT THE GAY AGENDA!*

She wasn't about to change, thanks. It was her United States, too. Her "gay agenda" was sunbathing and drinking iced coffee, just at the moment. She tried to relax into summer vacation, lying in the hammock in her backyard.

The Kona coffee was so good. The hammock supported her tired bicycling muscles. *I earned this. I taught an overload all year. I graded hundreds and hundreds of papers. Pretend I'm in Hawaii. Pretend I'm on vacation by the sea and the hammock is strung between two coconut palms. I'm sipping a Mai Tai.*

And I'm not alone, either. If only it were Gail lying beside her. Ah, was that so wrong, to miss her warm ex-partner? She closed her eyes, imagining snuggling into the familiar curves. Being held, holding. Holding. The pleasure of breathing together.

In her fantasy, their reunion didn't have to be sex. What she really missed were times like these, the body in its state of relaxation, her lover's nose nuzzling the back of her neck as innocent as a burrowing puppy. And then more. The nuzzling that led to soft lips opening to press against her shoulder. Shivering and taking in that simple love until she couldn't resist the impulse to shift and turn, to take that face in her two hands and drink deeply of familiar afternoon love. Gail.

The hammock, absolutely still. The coffee in her bloodstream, strong, sweet. Sweat building just at her hairline, behind her ears. Her hand caressing her bare thigh, the alert hawk in the tree high above her that she did not see with her closed eyes.

Gradually Gail became Isabel in her mind. Was that wrong? Was that so surprising? Who knew Hannah's moods as well as Isabel, now that Gail was gone these years? What was the magic her bartender friend wove in their community, after all? *Don't think. Feel. Let it in. Let somebody in while you can.* Isabel was there. Isabel breathed into her back, her hairline, her ear. Isabel's long nose touched her throat; her warm lips ever so gently met Hannah's chin. The scent of flowers, already strong in the summer yard, strengthened around the hammock, and suddenly grew more tropical. Plumeria, lilikoi, gardenia.

Hannah became aware of someone else's breath. From across the garden it came, carrying a strangely female heat. This breath was very warm, then warmer, insistent. Quickly, it had the strength of fire. She flinched. Then, to her alarm, a full steam began to burn her eyes. She sat up, thoughts of Isabel disrupted, fragmented. She heard, rather than felt, the breath of a song. A chunk of rock grazed her shoulder and she jumped out of the hammock, scrambling for cover.

Who was throwing rocks at her as she lay caressing herself in her rainbow hammock on the third of July? Who wanted to disturb her? Was it some homophobe from that conference?

She had been trying to avoid thoughts of that right-wing group, coming into the community to claim and ruin Independence Day with their hellfire and brimstone homophobia. Now hellfire and brimstone was raining into her yard. She bent to look at the rock that had nearly hit her. The grass there had turned black, singed. There it was: just a tiny piece of rock, but burning hot. Like lava.

The daydream had become a message. She knew what she had to do, beginning with putting on shoes. No sense burning her feet off, not when there was work to do. Vacation time would wait. Sighing, Hannah returned to the house.

Moira was cramming for the LSATs, hoping to become a lawyer for other lesbian veterans purged during Don't Ask, Don't Tell. She had locked herself into Sappho's Bar and Grill for the long weekend, studying for four or five hours at a stretch, then eating from the small high-energy plates Isabel served her, then napping, then studying again. When Hannah stormed into the bar, Moira was chanting the Constitution. "*We* the people, of the United States . . ."

"Yeah, I know—except a lot of those 'people' were left out of the Founding Fathers' playbook on full participation in a democracy. Look, I need your help. I'm, ah, I'm heading over to that church on Leroy. The one where they're having that conference? I'm going to, you know, write about it," Hannah tried to say casually. Moira raised one dark eyebrow.

"You're going to crash it, you mean. Is this some sort of protest? Trying to get arrested on Independence Day? Don't go to jail tonight, asshole. You'll miss the barbecue, the fireworks . . ."

"The *drinks*," Isabel added from behind the bar.

"No," Hannah fumbled. "I don't plan to make trouble. But I feel like I need to sit in it and take notes on what they're up to. As a historian of these times."

"Know thy enemy, huh? Nice idea, doc; but are you nuts? They'll spot you as an infiltrator in seconds." Moira put down her lawbook, amused, and studied Hannah with a critical eye. "I think you'd better have a makeover first."

"I know. Loan me a dress?"

Letty and Trale, who had up to that moment been engaged in a game of eight-ball, abruptly put down their cue sticks and began to laugh. "This I gotta see," Letty guffawed.

Dog, who styled hair for the Park Hotel salon, lit up like a firefly at the challenge before her. "Let me at you. Oh my God, a first. A first! Get the camera out, Moira. I think our dyka-demic's going to have to shave her legs."

"I'll go get my John Deere lawnmower then," from Letty.

"You'll need to look like a married wife," Isabel pointed out, coming from around the bar with a plate of fish tacos for Moira. "Here." She pulled a sparkling ring from one long finger and moved it onto Hannah's hand. For an instant, Hannah felt the breath of fire again, and the sensation of Isabel's lips on her throat. "Are we married, now?" she joked bashfully, but Isabel only smiled.

In no time at all, Hannah was pasted into a modest polyester suit skirt and blouse left over from last year's talent show revue at the bar, and, with a borrowed Bible and hairspray disguising her midsummer mullet, she walked determinedly up to the conference.

Why was she doing this? Maybe to hear exactly what was being said about her community. She was itchy from the sense of being maligned, misrepresented, and mocked during a holiday that celebrated freedom and democracy and independence from oppression. On the other hand, whose freedom did "Independence Day" celebrate? It did not emancipate the thousands of slaves already held in bondage in colonial America. It did not put

African women on an equal political footing with the Founding Fathers who bought, owned, and sold them—or, in the case of Thomas Jefferson, also fathered children with them. Women of any race failed to gain rights in the new U.S. Constitution. Native Americans were not helped by the Fourth of July. And yet these questions did not bother the good people gathering at the church on Leroy Street today. Their obsession was the threat women like Hannah posed to America's stability. Yet, dressed as she was now, passing as "straight," she was welcomed with broad smiles.

"Pray with me?" beamed an attractive conference host as soon as Hannah pushed open the lobby door, and Hannah found her hand gripped hard by a woman whose plump breasts were held together with a laminated *No Gay Agenda* pin. They stood together at a table covered with screamingly formatted *Homosexuals Can Change* pamphlets, Hannah screwing her eyes shut in what she hoped was a convincing imitation of prayer. *Pray I get through this.*

She took her seat amid hundreds of women, all shapes, sizes, skin colors, hair textures. Ironically, homophobia had succeeded in uniting the diversity of American womanhood where her own feminist community still struggled with outreach and inclusion. There were women of every race, age and ethnicity here, black and white, Latina, Pacific Islander, plus a few obvious lesbians sporting the lapel pins and shirt slogans of ex-gay ministries. Their sad, defensive glances scraped over her now, but no one recognized her personally. It seemed that everyone was from out of town, and just Hannah was local.

The panic that a former lover might be here among the converted continued to send fresh sweat to her belly. What would she do if a woman she'd once loved chose to reject "the lifestyle" and turned professional homophobe? This had already happened to some of Hannah's friends. Earlier that year, Carol's ex agreed to meet her for dinner and, excusing herself to use the bathroom, slipped into their old bedroom in order to tuck evangelical pamphlets under Carol's pillow.

Hannah took her seat in what was evidently a pew, her legs crawling beneath the unfamiliar nylons Moira had forced over her shaven legs. Between the sweat trickling into raw nicks, the binding nylon material, and the summer humidity mushrooming in the non-air-conditioned church hall, her legs felt like two throbbing tree trunks. Could anyone notice?

"I know," nodded a handsome black woman to her left. "*Hot* in here. But the flames of hell burn hotter for the unrepentant sinner. Are you saved, sister?"

"Um, sure," Hannah assented weakly. What was the etiquette? "Since 1979," she added in sly attribution to the year she had come out.

They can't tell. I could be anyone. With her hair pressed and the right outfit, a ring twinkling from her finger, she could pass, not only as straight and married but as Christian. As Gentile. How many other women had tried to pass, to survive? Butch women passing as men, Jews passing as not-Jewish during the Holocaust, light-skinned African Americans escaping slavery, Irish Catholic women needing work in Protestant locations. Sojourner Truth, an eloquent speaker, was once accused of being a man in disguise. Her accuser, a pro-slavery minister, demanded that she be examined to prove she was in fact female. She had ripped open her blouse, shouting "I will show my breasts to the entire congregation!" Harriet Tubman had passed as both an old man and an old woman, bound for market, when in fact there were escaping slaves rather than chickens in her retrofitted wagon. And one of Hannah's favorite class lectures involved Ellen Craft, a light-skinned runaway slave who escaped with her own husband by posing as his white, male owner.

There was power in the act and art of disguise. But it did not feel pleasant to think today of the thousands of gay kids growing up in these fundamentalist homes, pretending to be "normal" until they could get out.

The day's program unfolded with prayer, song, and several gifted public speakers. Having been to many a badly planned lesbian conference, Hannah had to admire the smooth rhetorical skills and tightly scheduled flow of featured presenters. No pause for a bathroom break or a Fourth of July cupcake interrupted the urgent calls to stop America's corruption by fiendish homosexuals. One woman after another rose to give her testimony. Yes, Christ's healing compassion must be shown to those trapped in this tragic and sinful lifestyle, but never forget that the Homosexual Agenda was a form of domestic terror, creeping in to destroy the family life and constitutional foundations of a Christian America. (Was Moira paying attention to this? wondered Hannah.) Homosexuals sought to overturn Western civilization, to deny all babies a mother and a daddy, to corrupt youth with perverse pedophilia instead of sanctified man-woman marriage. AIDS was the vengeance of the Lord. Praised be He.

Behind Hannah, the steady *thump* of a Bible accompanied each statement from the podium as a well-dressed white woman rhythmically pounded her agreement. Next to Hannah, another woman rose to ask the minister at the lectern, "They make me *sick*. Just what is it they want, Reverend?"

"They want *special rights*," thundered one of the few men in the assembled throng, a sour-faced hate radio personality Hannah had long hoped she would never meet in person. "They cannot ever, ever be a protected class, for their sin is the chosen behavior of the sinner! Never forget that the decadent homosexual is a successful minority in this land, and does not merit a law against discrimination. Why, the homosexual is among the wealthiest special-interest groups in America. Rich in the bank, if morally bankrupt!" he concluded with a flourish, and shouts of "Amen!" filled Hannah's ears.

It was too much. She thought of her friends at the bar: so many, like Moira, expelled from the military without benefits, thrown out by their own families, beaten, denied custody, institutionalized, queer-bashed, sick, homeless. No history of discrimination? No poverty? Their own churches (and synagogues, and mosques) had rejected them, offering cold comfort, if any. *And listen to what's preached at that microphone.* Parental rejection, which surely might count as discrimination, was energetically endorsed. Put that gay child out of the house. She saw this in her own students. No longer welcome at home, but too old for child protective services at eighteen, some had slept in the street until their college financial aid package arrived. Despite increasingly comprehensive gay rights laws, kids were still leaving small towns and taking the Greyhound bus to Greenwich Village and San Francisco for freedom, an invisible migration. Hannah's thoughts turned to the Great Migration just before and after World War I, when so many southern African Americans left impossible Jim Crow conditions for Northern city work. (And how many had been gay? And how many brought their loosed gay spirits to the Harlem Renaissance?)

"Ours is a Christian America, a beautiful America," ranted the minister, and the church choir on site launched into a soaring rendition of "America, The Beautiful."

Behind her, the woman who had thumped her Bible the loudest suddenly reached over the pew and grabbed Hannah's hand. Hannah felt the emotion in her grasp. The woman's hand was shaking, damp with perspiration—either with patriotic fervor or religious fervor, or perhaps both. Perhaps it was the political fervor of truly believing she was right and that a Christian America, devoid of nasty homosexuals, was *her* America. Hannah was singing, too, not only to ward off suspicion but because this was still a great anthem, the one she had always loved singing in elementary school. It saddened her to hear it now, used for such oppressive purpose. She longed to whisper fiercely at the woman gripping her hand, "It's *our America, too!*"

It was only after this phrase crossed her mind that Hannah realized she was holding the hand of another lesbian. Had she been dragged, right then, into a court of law or before her God (church and state, she reflected wryly), in no way she could have sworn with truth just how she knew. But the energy had changed. A sister was behind her. And that meant that someone else had infiltrated. Was passing. Who was she?

Before she could turn around and risk grateful, curious eye contact, the woman let go of Hannah and rose up standing, as giant as a tree, and on the last pious notes of "America the Beautiful" she thundered out, "Ladies and gentlemen: If you please, I wrote that song." Heads turned, mouths gaped, the pianist fell off her stool, and the woman held them all in her burning gaze. "I am Katharine. I am Katharine Lee Bates."

Next to her, a dark-skinned woman threw off her veil, revealing kinky Hawaiian hair, and she sang out, "I am Queen Liliokalani, and I wrote *Aloha O'e*, 'Farewell to Thee,' as your missionaries invaded my island and in the name of your God put me under house arrest. I wrote an anthem, too. Will you not sing it?"

And the elegant black woman who had asked Hannah if she'd been saved now tossed aside her own prayer book and said, "I am Sally Hemings, the real mother of this nation. Your founding father fondled me, and had his children, unclaimed, through me as his slave. His white wife, my half-sister, *owned me*. In his life Thomas Jefferson fathered children through me while never granting me Emancipation. I am your traditional family values. I am your Constitution. Look at me."

And a plump white woman at the end of their row sighed and rose on creaking knees, and added: "I am Abigail, and nothing I said mattered, though you read my letters even to this day. I am Abigail Adams. I begged my husband to remember the ladies, to form a government fair to women's power. Do you think women's voices must only rise in hymn? To Him? Where is *Her* America?"

Katharine swept to the front of the room and faced the choir, telling them, "It is time *you* faced the music, my dear ones. I have loved women since I was but a girl, writing in my diary even as a child that 'I like women better than men.' For the span of my adult life I loved another woman, whose name was also Katharine, and in that nineteenth century, mind you, I wrote to her with desire. I wrote to her 'I want you so much my Dearest, and I want to love you so much better than I have ever loved.' Will you not teach that, too, in every one of your so-called Christian schools where you sing my song?"

Queen Lil pointed now at Hannah. "Do not ever forget this is not *my* Independence Day, *wahine. Haole.* Yes, you teach the history of Katharine's woman-love. But still you exoticize *me.* Only yesterday you drank my coffee, feeling free, lying in that hammock, thinking that your hard work merits a vacation in my Hawa'ii. And my hard work? My woman's home? If, lying in that hammock, you had just looked to the left in your mind's eye. If you had looked just past your fantasy, you'd see my palace. There. They kept me under house arrest. I had to send Pele to wake you up, to graze you with the fire of her wrath. It was not Christian land, my lovely island. It was raped by Christians, dressed by missionaries, planted, seized . . ." She broke off.

"As I was planted," said Hemings. "As I was owned."

In the stunned silence, with the choir agog, no one from the Take Back the United States conference spoke. Then the four leaders for the day's event knelt together with eyes squeezed shut and began to chant ritually, "Pray away the gay. Pray away the gay."

All eyes were closed and all lips moving as Bates, Hemings, Adams, and the Queen swept up and out, Hannah trailing in their glorious wake. The church door slammed.

"Don't worry. They will not remember any of this," said Sally. "These people are very good at forgetting, at not seeing what they don't care to believe." But she smiled briefly.

"Here's the thing," said Abigail. "We do not all know one another. We are always starting from that same point, thinking we alone must do all of the work. We fail to work together, do we not?" Her eyes pierced Hannah, who quickly responded, "We don't all know one another in my time, either."

"Let's get away for a moment," suggested Katharine. "We don't have much time. We won't be seen if we keep moving." A cart rumbled up to the church steps then—an actual horse-drawn cart layered with quilts, the driver's face hidden behind an enormous sunbonnet.

"Get in," growled the driver. "Gentle now."

Hannah watched as her new companions delicately arranged

90

their cumbersome garments while climbing into the wagon. These were the clothes of colonization women had been forced to wear in the nineteenth century, introduced in Hawaii by zealous missionaries, and eventually a normal part of everyday discomfort, particularly in high summer, as now. The "Mother Hubbard" dresses given to the islanders. Corsets in Katharine's day. School uniforms, gloves and stockings, petticoats, tightly buttoned sleeves. How had women survived, labored in fields and kitchens, endured cramps and wounds, given birth, reigned and resisted, in such garb?

"White clothes," said Lil, nodding to Sally. "They will weigh you down. In water, they will drown you."

"You will not know true liberation until a *woman* undresses you," Katharine assured. Abigail blushed beet red.

The wagon pulled away from the church steps, and Hannah looked behind her to see if their odd group was visible to the other conference guests still arriving. "Of course not," said Sally Hemings, reading her mind. "No one sees women's history. I'm barely acknowledged by Jefferson's family, my children yet unclaimed by his descendants. Mixed-race women? In plain sight, yet invisible. Watch." And indeed the wagon drove right through the first traffic intersection, apparently unseen.

Hannah felt a sharp rapping under her feet. The wagon bed planking was rattling with an urgency out of rhythm with the turning of the wheels. A voice spoke below her knees. One faint word, but clear. "*Moses.*" Then she gasped as four tiny brown fingers reached up through a plank knothole and seized her hand.

There were women and children hidden in the hay, in the false bottom of the wagon. It could only mean that the driver was Harriet Tubman. And when Hannah raised her head, Leroy Street had disappeared. They were on a country road, abundant with pines. And gaining on their party was a smartly appointed coach with a parson at the reins.

Abigail clamped her hand around Hannah's wrist. "*Notwithstanding all your wise Laws and Maxims we have it in our power not only to free ourselves but to subdue our Masters.*"

"That and more," agreed Hemings. "Didn't you also tell your husband, 'If particular care and attention is not paid to the Laidies we are determined to foment a rebellion, and will not hold ourselves bound by any Law in which we have no voice, or Representation'?"

"I did. But our husbands had peculiar ideas about freedom."

"Forget husbands altogether," advised Katharine. "Anyone who enslaved his own kids has failed to love mercy more than life." She grew quiet as the parson's coach drew up alongside them. Liliokalani inhaled.

"Blessed day!" said the minister. "I am alert for six runaways, two wenches and their young. Have you had sight of them?"

"I am well known for not supporting your Constitution," answered the Queen, and Hannah heard a snort of laughter from the well-disguised Tubman in the driving seat of their wagon. Hannah realized that it was important to keep talking, to mask any possible sounds of the children below. "Sir, may we move on?" she heard herself. "We're, um . . . bound for market day." She felt rather than heard a child's cough under her feet.

"Who is your husband?" demanded the preacher.

"She is *not married,*" Katharine snarled.

"And yet you have a wedding ring!" the man persisted. "Or does that, too, belong to another? Is that, too, missing property?" He leaned closer, the rancid smell of sweaty black broadcloth almost under Hannah's nose. She flinched. She'd forgotten about Isabel's ring!

"A pox on your ideas of ownership," said Hemings, and tapped Tubman on the shoulder with her elegant glove. "Drive, Moses. Drive." And the horse leapt forward.

"Where are we going?" Hannah begged. And the great Harriet Tubman turned from her perch atop their racing wagon, and answered: "Don't you know? We're going *Underground.*"

"God shed Her grace, crowned thy good with sisterhood," Bates screamed at the slaveowner, now far behind them in the dust. Queen Lil pulled up the planking with one mighty arm, and the hidden family groups emerged from their hay-strewn recesses, breathing in the fresh air.

"Drive," shouted Hemings. "Get me out of here. Emancipate us all."

A circle of women and children looked at Hannah. "Are we bound for freedom now?" asked a girl.

"Nobody is BOUND anymore," came tossed from the driver's seat.

"How will we live?" whispered one woman, and Sally Hemings seized Hannah's hand and said, "You will have to sell that ring. That will feed us all."

"It's not mine; it's Isabel's," Hannah tried to explain, and Bates crowed, "Aha. A sister! So, she is your companion?" "No—" Hannah began again, but the dust was swirling thickly, and she found it hard to raise her voice. Then it was actually hard to breathe. She shut her eyes, clearing her throat, coaxing it to relax. She heard the children coughing also. "Water," they cried.

Hemings had her elegant hand clamped like a vise on Hannah's. "Listen to these, my children," she hissed. "Is there no greater suffering on the Cross than their thirst? Which of your pious pastors would bear honest witness to *that* crucifixion?"

The sun was setting. It was almost dusk. There was a sudden lurch of the wagon and then, abruptly, they turned into a shadowy lane with overhanging trees, heavy with midsummer flowers. Just ahead, beyond the curve of older, dried wagon tracks, Hannah could see a barn.

"All out," called Tubman. "This is the safe house. Quick now." The families moved swiftly, unfolding limbs, barely pausing to shake off dust before disappearing into the hayloft, as a tall black woman in a green bonnet hurried toward them. She smiled deeply, gesturing to ritual foods laid out on a rough-hewn table in the barn. "You made it into freedom territory. Come and eat. Welcome!"

Hannah turned to ask her companions *What Now*, only to find that Queen Lil and Abigail had vanished altogether, and Katharine and Sally were lost in conversation. "They will never tell the truth about our partners," Katharine murmured.

"It's the job of the historian," agreed Sally. They looked at

Hannah. Yes, she taught their truths in class. She read their lives late into the night all winter long, marveling and outraged. Had she done right by them? How much gratitude and respect could she express for their daring, their realities? There could never be enough.

"Come and eat. All are welcome here," their host was calling, but in a low voice, ever watchful. "Come and eat, and lay your burden down."

Lay your burden down. Hannah knew there was no earthly comparison to the actual flight from slavery, no appropriating the safe stations of the Underground Railroad in thinking about the flight from homophobia. But leaving that Take Back America meeting and its "homosexual agenda" sermons had reminded her that millions of gay kids were still working their way out of mental enslavement. Finding a way out of shame and punitive religious teachings was a different kind of flight and migration— and Hannah's classroom was a safe station for gay youth leaving the evangelical authorities who had thundered against their lives. And what had Hannah's safe station been? The Michigan festival? Hadn't she laid her burden down there, at nineteen, in those fields of woman celebrating?

Hannah never reached the barn. Tubman turned one last time and looked at her, tipped the male farmer's hat of her passing disguise, and melted into the night. The planks of the wagon coagulated into leatherette bus seats. The driver of the Greyhound was a gray-haired Amazon in uniform cotton shirt and crisp-creased pants. The neon sign above the steering wheel shimmered *Grand Rapids, Michigan.* The rows stretched back, four deep, filled with the hearty-shaped ghosts of every woman Hannah had known in festival culture who had passed to the beyond. Maxine Feldman was talking with Kay Gardner. Leslie Feinberg was arguing with Margaret Sloan-Hunter. Therese Edell was strumming a guitar. But next to Hannah in the hot bus seat was a very alive and buff young Asian woman, perhaps eighteen, nervously snacking from a Tupperware container of kimchi. "I'm almost there," she whispered.

"What? Where? Who are you?" Hannah almost wailed, craning her head to identify anything familiar, and encountering the welcome wink of deceased dykes she had flirted with at festivals. "Where are we *going?*"

"I'm Grace; I'm going to the festival. I just got away from a Christian intervention camp. You know, they take gay kids, and try to deprogram you? It was so horrible, so scary. But I had a friend who rescued me when I went into town to do the laundry. She got me this bus ticket and even brought me comfort food." Grace gestured with her chopstick. "I'm never going back! I'm never sitting through another sermon telling me I'm sick. I'm never going to be paddled again by my parents and my pastor. I'm free!" She looked at Hannah, who of course was still in her church clothes. "You made it out, too!" And now Hannah recognized the teenager from the miserable ex-gay group of guests back at church conference she'd attended. Was it just earlier that day?

"Here," Grace invited. "Have some of my lunch. Come on and eat. We're free now! We're going to *Michfest,* with thousands of other lesbians, and we're gonna take our shirts off!" And the bus jerked to a halt at the roadside to let aboard Ruth Ellis, who had attended festivals well into her nineties and died at age 100, and the ghosts of lesbian freedom shouted hello. The driver glanced at them in her rear-view mirror, and her eyes were the eyes of Harriet Tubman, of Katharine Lee Bates, and then the eyes of twentieth-century heroines: Barbara Gittings, Gladys Bentley. And then she was Deborah Sampson. Sampson, who had disguised herself as a male to fight in the American Revolution. Wounded in battle, she removed the bullet herself so no surgeon could reveal her secret. She had fought for freedom and healed herself.

As they all had, Amazons all.

Then their mercurial-eyed driver shifted the gear of the mighty bus and it leaped forward, forward. They were bound for freedom in a land they could not yet see. The huge wheels left the ground, and the bus took wing and flew. No turning back. No fear.

"You made it. Come and eat. Welcome!" It was Isabel's voice, Isabel gently removing the ring from her hand, and Hannah sputtered out dust and inhaled, gasping. "Here." Isabel held a glass of lemonade to her lips. The shadowy figures around Hannah turned into Yvette, Moira, Dog, Letty, and Trale, and the scent of potato salad rose from a picnic table. They were in the parking lot outside of Sappho's Bar and Grill, with the first town fireworks breaking loudly overhead and hoots of excitement from the tank top-wearing tomboys gathered for holiday barbecue.

"But what—Tubman, in her wagon—that bus to Michigan. Wait, are we safe here?" Hannah mumbled, stupefied, and her friends gazed quizzically back at her, until Moira relaxed into an expression of understanding. "Yeah, you went to that revival thing! Still in that outfit, too, huh? I'd be shell-shocked myself. Relax; let's get you changed. But look who followed you here. Here where it's safe."

Standing behind the long barbecue table was the young, buff Asian woman Hannah recognized from the mystery bus she'd just been riding, from the "ex-gay" group at the conference. They blinked at one another. "Hello," said the guest. "I'm gay. I mean, I'm Grace." Isabel walked over and dropped her ring into Grace's lemonade glass, and then just once, swiftly, ran a finger around the rim, which released a humming, singing noise. It released the music notes of an old anthem. Much older than the one by Katharine Lee Bates.

Shivering, despite the very warm evening, Hannah peeled off her borrowed church clothes and reassembled herself, adding layer by familiar layer until she was in her favorite and free-wheeling clothes: surfing jams, Lesbian Equality T-shirt. She looked down at the faux-Polynesian pattern on her surf shorts and reflected that the design, the concept, the association of surfing as freedom had all been seized for Americans from Queen Liliokalani's time. That the woman-loving equality in her shirt slogan had been lived out more than a hundred years earlier by the educated lesbian who penned "America, The Beautiful," and that Independence Day had done nothing to free the slaves or advance women's rights in the new Constitution, just as Abigail Adams had predicted. Thomas Jefferson had gladly written of freedom as that which man could not live without, fathering a nation while simultaneously fathering children through a young slave woman he owned. Freedom: It had trickled down incrementally to the women of America through time—women who had not dared to know each other, who had been told that God forbade their speaking out.

But now the path to freedom was a path for gay rights, too. The binding power of religion was loosening in her own era, despite the angry rally she had infiltrated today. Hannah looked at Grace, beaming over the barbecue, newly released from the folly of trying to be *ex-gay*. Grace was wearing Isabel's ring, which had turned into a freedom ring with rainbow gems sparkling from her brown hand. And Grace nodded toward her and said, "You don't have to go too far to find new family. I'm finding it at Sappho's, just like you."

Chapter Eight
Labor Day Weekend

Heading home from the festival each August was always like crossing an unmarked seasonal threshold from summer into fall.

No matter how hot and humid the last night of festival concerts might be, with steam visibly rising from exposed bodies as women danced at the edge of the stage, the next morning the air would change to sharp autumn gloss. That first feeling of the coming fall was a tang and a tentacle that curled delicately around festiegoers as each made her farewells. Teachers packing up tents, bedrolls, and raingear felt their antennae go up: School was coming. Soon.

Inevitably, returning to town via the parkway that hugged the hillside, the first thing Hannah noticed was the discount drugstore's banner: *Back to School Special!* The bars along Clinton Street, both seedy and upscale, threw out their sandwich boards with beckoning words: *Happy Hour College Specials. Welcome Back Students. We I.D.* Awaiting her on campus would be six inches of mail, and little blue notices in her faculty mailbox such as "Your fall textbook order is incomplete. The campus bookstore regrets to report that the textbook you ordered for Women's History 001 is out of print and unavailable for the fall semester." And so forth. The distance from festival euphoria to sheer academic panic was a very fast crossing.

As always, upon arriving home from two weeks of camping at a lesbian festival, Hannah flopped gratefully across her soft double bed, stretched her back and legs in every direction her pup tent had not allowed, and then plowed through the refrigerator. Holding her overstuffed sandwich in one hand, she examined her face in the bathroom mirror. Tanned, burnished skin and clear eyes gazed back. There were ferns in her hair, several crushed mosquitoes baked into the back of her neck. Her double women's symbol necklace swung low between sunburnt breasts that had been nowhere near a bra since July. Soon they'd be encased behind a teaching blazer, the recently lived-out fantasy of nude camping in women-only space fading into memory as fall classes began. She'd exchange the tofu-flecked veggie stews and potato soups of festival cuisine for her hastily assembled sandwiches and the heart-recharging coffee of the campus cafeteria. Her topless tan and toughened muscles would go unseen, untouched. She still had no lover in town.

Sighing, Hannah began to pull rain-sodden shorts and sweatshirts from her duffel bag, dividing up the pungent gear into neatly apportioned laundry loads. First laundry. Then a shower *and* an herbal bath soak. Twigs and spider legs would swirl out of her hair, disappearing forever into the drain as she transformed from forest Medusa to bespectacled dykademic. Then up to campus to lose her cool in the bookstore, wailing about how to replace the out-of-print readings that were never going to arrive. Should she give up asking her students to purchase real books and just go digital, with all her women's history assignments online, as other professors did nowadays? Why did it feel like such a betrayal to read Virginia Woolf on glass? Could there ever be a cyber equivalent word for *bookworm?*

But just below the fresh layer of anxiety, there was that glorious fire of recommitment, a feeling she recognized with gratitude and pleasure. The festival had once again fired her up to embrace her chosen work, examining the words of women's lives. In spite of the enormous workload, she still loved the cycle of the academic year, its curving arc of predictability ingrained since she was four and had started nursery school. The weather obligingly shifted to cool; *kneesock weather,* her mother used to say, meaning it was time to put away the shorts and bathing suits of summer play and pull on socks and saddle shoes for school. Hannah would beg and plead for just a few more days of running through the sprinkler, shirtless, free, unselfconscious, wearing her favorite pair of orange cutoffs, her threadbare P.F Flyers tennis shoes. But school also meant books when she was young and coming to realize how different she was from other little kids. Hannah's kickball-playing pals had hated library day, whereas Hannah found it heavenly. Now she was a grownup, and could read all day, every day, and not be considered a freak because it *was her job* to read. She had earned the freedom to be forever at home in history class, her mental pencil box rattling, her heart and soul engaged.

By Sunday of Labor Day weekend Hannah was giddy with pre-paredness and back-to-school nostalgia, scuffing new loafers through a few early-turned and scattered leaves. She was on her way to Sappho's for a last, lazy afternoon of watching baseball on the big screen Isabel had just installed, looking forward to sipping a brew with some of the big gals who were knowledge-able sports fanatics. Too soon, Labor Day weekend would be over and Hannah would be possessed by the demands of new students, by lectures to prepare, by hours spent with her nose in a textbook, deciphering the great women of history—including those figures from the past whom she was somehow starting to *run into,* in the oddest of ways. Hannah took a long and winding route, walking to Sappho's instead of driving so that she was free to ponder. What were these women from history trying to tell her, or show her?

"Watch it, jerk face! You're going to hit that lady!" Hannah jumped off the curb as a worn baseball banged her ankle. It rolled off her shoe, downhill into a side street, and two sheepish-looking little girls who had erred in a game of catch stood mortified but giggling in their front yard, awaiting Hannah's reaction. The bigger of the two girls, twisting her finger around beaded braids, ventured: "Are you okay?"

"I'm fine. You missed my soft parts." They doubled over with hilarity at that. Hannah approached the barefoot pair, hand extended to show she wasn't mad. "I'm actually on my way to watch a baseball game myself. I love to see girls practicing; keep it up! Either of you know how to pitch a curve ball?"

The bigger girl glanced at her companion, who was white and red-headed and wearing a backwards-turned ball cap. "*She* thinks I can. My dad says I can't and never will. See, all we got at my school is slow-pitch softball. No baseball because there's no one to coach the girls."

"Well, there ought to be!" Hannah snarled, her feminist avatar uncoiling and rising like a cobra; and the girls involuntarily took a step back. "You know, there's a *law* that says girls can do any sport boys do. It's called—"

"Title IX," the redhead volunteered. "My mom's a lawyer."

Hannah looked at the sharp-featured little face, recognizing the dimples. "Your mom wouldn't be Elaine Grady, would she?"

"Ha, Susie's got *two* moms," the first girl said. "Now, how fair is that? I don't even have one. My mama died."

Susie frowned. "Shut up, Cubby. Yes, Elaine is my mom, but so is—"

"—Denise," finished Hannah. "Guess what: I know both of them. Okay. Susie, tell your mom Elaine to talk with Cubby's school principal, and I bet you can get a girls' baseball team started over there. It's been done before, you know? Grownup women played hardball once. They were really good, too. In this league during World War II—"

"Yeah, *A League of Their Own*," Susie interrupted. "We watched that movie at my ninth birthday party in May."

"But it had just white girls," Cubby pointed out. "There was that one lady who could throw a curve and they wouldn't even let her into that ballpark."

The three of them stood there awkwardly, until Susie broke the silence. "Can you please go get our baseball for us? I think it rolled downhill behind you. We're not supposed to leave Cubby's front yard while her daddy's napping."

"Oh. Right." Hannah hurried after the lost ball, thinking, *These kids know more than my own students. They don't need me to pitch lectures on women's history; they need female coaches who can pitch them curve balls. I'll have to get our asshole athletic director at the university to shift money around and bring in a personal trainer for Cubby, ideally someone who knows the history of women in the Negro Leagues—But* . . . Then she stopped cold, feeling her bruised ankle throb as her heart sped up. The ball had rolled all the way down the block and vanished into Willow Street. And Hannah had not turned the corner into that street in fourteen years.

She drove past it all the time, mentally chanting *Don't look. Keep going.* Everyone had a street, she supposed, where the perfect love affair had played out, the architecture of a house and a street number containing the entire world of a finished relationship. In her own imagination it had never changed, that narrow townhouse, its yellow door opening right onto the old stone street, with a carriage lamp and a window box heavy with zinnias. She had never talked about it with Gail, who didn't like to know about Hannah's past with other women. But Isabel knew, and Isabel would remember—that Hannah had once loved a woman on Willow Street. She had loved the visiting scholar named Maud Nora.

It was right after Hannah finished her Ph.D., when she joined the university as a freshly minted young professor. They met over the wine and cheese at a reception for new faculty, talking about their heavy teaching loads and how to tackle it all, at different ages, different professional stages—Hannah with her new place in the world of women's history and Maud, older, better known, brought in for two years of special seminars on women's sports and culture. It was the busy expert Maud who introduced Hannah to the history of the All American Girls Professional Baseball League. Maud even had an Aunt Marlene, nicknamed

"Lumpy" for the bump on her head from a particularly rough game, who briefly played second base for the Grand Rapids Chicks.

And Maud—that had been a romance so all consuming, Hannah barely remembered anything else about her first year of real employment. Yes, it was thrilling to stand at a lectern and watch students take notes, thrilling to take home a paycheck that soon turned into a leather jacket, a mountain bike, a complete set of Fiestaware, but most of that year was lost to kissing and waiting, kissing and waiting to kiss. With their equally demanding schedules, on some days they didn't see one another at all. On others—magic days, thought Hannah now—Hannah was allowed to spend the night, leaving her grubby first apartment for the luxury of Maud's rented townhouse. They'd meet in that gold doorway, their leather satchels bumping. With a jingle of her keys, Maud would jab the door open and pour herself a glass of wine and settle on the couch with her half-glasses so charmingly askew, pretending to grade a few more student papers until the sexual tension wound up between them like a spring. Then Hannah had to pounce, to throw herself beseechingly into that waiting lap and bury her lips in Maud's cable knit sweater, the Celtic wool a fuzzbite in her teeth as Maud's own breathing quickened. On the sofa they made love while dusk began to gather, kids coming in from street games of baseball then, too, and cats yowling for their evening meal, and the train that rumbled every night at five. Eventually, on those special nights, Hannah would sigh and pull away and start a sauce for pasta in the narrow old kitchen with the butcher block island somehow fitting in between them, and Maud would watch the news while chopping vegetables or stripping husks off corn, and then by eight they'd eat their meal with jazz or blues or Bach—or women's music. Maud had every album ever made by any feminist musician, crates she'd brought with her from Ann Arbor along with a real stereo turntable and diamond-tipped needle. On such nights she'd raise her glass and say, "To my young scholar," toasting Hannah with one foot beneath the table stroking hers. That narrow house creaked and listed, groaned in autumn wind and froze them in the winter, so that Maud was often sick and Hannah was always steaming her with pots of tea, with herbal decongestants, though Maud drew the line at "being vaporized," saying it sounded like a World War I attack. One night they both were bundled up in flannel, grading tests. Hannah had her hair down and her bathrobe loosely tied, and looked up with the feeling Maud was watching, and she was. "Jesus Christ," said Maud, "you certainly are a beauty," and then laid her glasses down. They went to bed. But it didn't last. *It never does,* thought Hannah bitterly.

It didn't last because Maud merely went back to her tenured position in Ann Arbor, where she was closer to the archives and living survivors of the League, and while they traveled back and forth to see one another for a few months, eventually Maud made clear with firm regret that she was "done." Hannah had raged and puzzled and written bad poetry, trying to figure out what could have turned Maud away. The answer eventually proved to be a hunky umpire named Daniel, who was also interested in the history of women's sports. He apparently owned a complete set of original AAGPBL trading cards and spent his weekends trolling flea markets for rare women's baseball memorabilia.

Left for a man. Left for a *man!* "Do you love *him,* or just his baseball card collection?" were Hannah's plaintive last words; it still hurt. The humiliation, on top of heartbreak, had ruined the very sight of the turnoff into Willow Street, which once excited her beyond description. She never again entered the street containing "their" house, not even when another faculty friend who lived farther down the block invited her to a holiday eggnog party. Maud's unexpected bisexuality was probably one reason why Hannah had eventually become involved with Gail, the butchest possible rebound partner; their first date lasted for so many happy years. But then Gail had walked out. Gail was gone, too.

Fuck it. Whatever. Hannah stepped into Willow Street, eyes focused on scooping up the children's lost ball, eyes blurry now with regret. Her hand shook as she touched the baseball. She wanted to touch Maud. She wanted to touch Gail. She wanted to go back in time and try again, forgive, apologize, be a better lover, anything at all. And as she turned at last to face the past, which was in this instance a townhouse at 307 Willow, another baseball came falling out of the sky and hit her on the head.

"Is she all right?"

"I don't know. *Marlene!* Can you get up?"

"Give her air. Come on, Gertie, shove over!"

Hannah opened an eye. For a moment she couldn't focus. Tense faces hovered over her—all topped with ball caps. She recognized nobody. But she heard a cheer go up, and for some reason scattered applause. "Hot damn, she's okay! Atta girl. Come on, get back in the game! It's so close!" Hands reached to lift her to her feet.

"Something hit me," began Hannah, and then gasped as she looked down at her bare legs. They were covered in bruises and scabs she hadn't had when she woke up that day. More distressingly, her legs seemed to be emerging from a skirt. A short uniform skirt. One she knew very well.

Hannah was a second basewoman for the Grand Rapids Chicks.

And that meant the year was 1945.

The sun was in the exact same position overhead, and the air had the same end-of-summer scent, but the women now pushing her toward second base had never known an IPad, e-mail, Skype, cell phone, even a television. Their chipped and crooked teeth, unrepaired by modern orthodontics, now smiled at her encouragingly. "Go on, we need you! Doreen's already out with a sprain. Can you play?"

"Can I play baseball? Hardball? Not well," Hannah stammered.

"That's the stuff. If Marlene's joking again, she can play. *Come on!* We still have a lead." Hannah found herself wobbling, on legs with unfamiliar sliding strawberries, toward a spot in a dirt field.

"Hurry up, princess," jeered an obvious dyke in a different color uniform skirt. "I didn't bean you that hard." At the slur *princess,* which in Hannah's world had always been the unflattering term for a spoiled Jewish girl, Hannah forgot her dizziness and whirled around, eyes shooting cinders, teeth grinding. She heard one of the players who had helped her up shout, "Yeah! There's that game face! Come on now, Marlene!"

I'm not Marlene. I'm Hannah. Who's Marlene? A base hit snapped her to attention as dust flew and a sliding opponent landed with a thud on first. "Son of an ITCH, that stung," the player moaned, and a shortstop from Hannah's team snorted in sympathy. "She can't risk another fine for swearing. The last swear cost her ten dollars, and a third gets her suspended from the League. That's Gloria—already busted for trying to go into one of those bars. Can't say as I blame her," she added, winking.

This is insane, Hannah thought, frantically fielding the next batter and missing the line drive by a country mile as the rival team advanced around the bases. Marlene, Marlene, I know that name. An ancient plane (to Hannah's eyes) sputtered over the field, dragging a banner that read WELL DONE TROOPS. Wait! Of course. Marlene was the name of Maud's aunt—the one who had actually played in the All American Girls Professional Baseball League. The one who got hit in the head at a game and carried a permanent lump on her temple that Maud had loved to pat as a little girl. Maud, who was much older than Hannah, who remembered and loved the League because she even went to a few games until her aunt finally retired in 1953.

What had Maud told Hannah about her aunt during the days and nights they lived together? Hannah had worked very hard to repress those happy memories, but she sure needed them now. It was on that frosty January night when they made cinnamon popcorn, their hands plunging into a hot-buttered bowl, knuckles bumping, lips salty-sweet and slippery, kernels falling into their laps, and Hannah's eyes had been on their rented horror

107

movie while Maud reminisced. What had she said, exactly, that night? "My aunt was probably a very gay lady, but they were barely allowed to talk about such things, let alone act on them. Five-dollar first offenses were handed out for cursing, smoking, drinking, wearing hair in too butch a bob, getting off the travel bus without your skirt on, even just wearing slacks in a public place. Oh, my aunt hated those rules, but she needed to keep every nickel of her earnings to help out the family farm, which was still recovering from the whammo of the Depression years. Marlene could whistle through her teeth—she never got the gap fixed, the way most kids do now—and she had a special whistle for me if she knew I was in the bleachers watching. She'd whistle twice during a lull in the action so I'd know she was thinking of me, and after the game we'd have Cracker Jacks together. Later on I recall that she usually had a woman friend with her, but of course when I was four, five, six, even twelve, I didn't put two and two together. After all, everyone on the team was a woman. And then they all had nicknames for each other, Slats, Mac, whatever. She was Lumpy, from being beaned with a ball one game. She always said it was her piece of history."

Hannah tried to clear her throbbing head. The uniform ball cap at least shielded her eyes. She could clearly see the people in the stands, some in military uniforms, others in clean overalls or house dresses—just white people, too, she noticed, and certainly no one was texting or talking on a cell phone. No one had on headphones, ear buds, or Nike swooshes. There were plenty of kids, cheering and waving, mostly young girls—

And one of the little girls was Maud Nora.

Definitely. It was Maud, or rather a pint-sized incarnation of her scholarly ex, who on this last weekend of summer 1945 would have been about to enter first grade. She had on a short-sleeved sweater buttoned up the wrong way, a plaid skirt, and Mary Janes. Her fair hair was pulled back with a yarn ribbon, and Cracker Jack glaze smeared her upper lip. She was screaming. "GO, Aunt Marlene, GO." Peanuts flew out of her mouth as she cheered.

Hannah parted her lips, afraid to say anything at all that might change the course of both their histories, but suddenly two quick and piercing whistles escaped from between her teeth. Mini-Maud shouted and waved at her. Hannah's head still throbbed from where she'd been knocked out—or, rather, knocked into the past and, apparently, into someone else's body, but when she reached up to touch her brow she was surprised to feel a cut and not a bump. *Hold on. If I'm "Lumpy," where's the lump? Or am I not Maud's aunt after all?*

"That's the game! We won! So long, Daisies!" shouted a player, and teammates from the Grand Rapids Chicks poured into the infield, whooping and cheering, while sullen Fort Wayne Daisies picked up their gloves and moved toward the waiting buses. In the bleachers, a little girl was waving, waiting. On legs that felt watery, yet real—there was no denying that she was alive and walking—Hannah approached young Maud.

The kid was five and a half. Not even a loose tooth yet. Probably couldn't read, either. Her life was ahead of her: school, high school, college, graduate school, peace marches, feminism, coming out, scholarship on women's sports, tenure at Ann Arbor, a fling with a younger woman named Hannah, partnering with an umpire named Daniel with a good baseball card collection. There was no reason to approach such a tiny figure with resentment, or to horrify her by spilling the beans about a future she had yet to live. Hannah was mindful that anything she said or did now that deviated in any way from Maud Nora's precise recollections would change history, and probably wreak havoc with Hannah's own life somewhere out there—if she ever got back to it. She stood awkwardly on one leg, pulling her uniform bloomers down an inch, saying nothing.

"I saved you my Cracker Jack prize," babbled Maud. "I almost swallowed it. Then I didn't." It was a very tiny silver baseball glove. "Perfect for you, huh?" And she held it out.

Hannah took it from the sticky hand, thinking, *This is a child*, thinking, *I am touching the hand that once held mine forty-five years later in time*, thinking, *How I loved that hand.* Could she say to little Maud what grown-up Maud had meant to her? "I love you, pal," was what Hannah used to say in the dark; and that phrase came out easy now. And little Maud responded: "I love *you!* You're my *best!*", the very thing older Maud had told Hannah in the dark.

Maybe that was all she had ever hoped to hear again, one more time, because Hannah/Marlene's body flooded with nostalgia, and she felt a grin crinkle all the way up to her cut forehead. In seconds, their meeting was over. A teammate pulled Hannah from the stands, saying "Come on, we gotta *go,*" and little Maud was shouting, "I'll see ya, Aunt Marlene! I'll see ya! I'll see ya next game!" And out in the parking lot, safely hidden behind the idling team bus, Hannah sank to her knees in the soft dirt and wept.

The next thing she knew she was dozing on the bus, its leather seats cracked and slippery, giving off a rank smell of liniment, cheap perfume, hair spray, and stale Coca-Cola. Someone was whispering in her ear: "When we stop for dinner, we can try to find that bar I heard about. We got maybe an hour. I really want to get a drink, but we'll have to be super careful or there's hell to pay, you know. So are you with me? Are you in?"

Up ahead, a truck stop parking lot, half-filled with very old farm Fords and pickups, beckoned with lights spelling out DON'S EATS in sputtering aqua neon. Twenty tired, victorious Chicks tugged on clean uniform skirts and filed off the bus toward the diner, but Hannah's companion shouted, "I'll be back in a bit. I'm gonna take old Marlene to the restroom to touch up that bruise!" She guided Hannah toward the side of the parking lot, then hustled past the freestanding bathroom toward a street glistening with trolley tracks.

"Where are you taking me?" wailed Hannah, desperate to fall asleep and wake up back on her way to Sappho's, in her own time and in her own body, but her teammate had other plans. They passed houses with sagging porches, and then crossed the tracks to an unpaved side street. Shapes of women and bawdy laughter drew them on toward one faintly lit brick house, its shades drawn.

"Just a bar, just a party Gina heard about," hissed her companion. Then as they reached the bottom step of the house, the front door opened and two beautifully dressed women reeled out. One had on a silk dress, pastel stockings well-seamed up the back, and a twisted pearl necklace. The other woman was in a pinstriped suit and sharp-brimmed fedora.

"Awesome," Hannah heard herself exclaim, before she remembered that was an expression very much from the future, marking her an alien. At the very same moment her seatmate from the bus yelled out, "Marlene, come back! Gina made a mistake! God damn it, that's a *colored* bar!"

The women on the porch were black.

"Who you calling God-damn colored?" said the butch in the fedora, casually but steadily taking the porch steps toward the rapidly receding Grand Rapids Chicks. "You too pretty to drink with us?" She looked at Hannah. "You two in that lily league? The white girls' ball league?"

The woman in the silk dress pointed a perfectly manicured middle finger at Hannah. "Pico's a better player than any of you. Think she could get on a League team? Uh uh. So why don't you go find some lily house party, and leave us our own spot?"

"It's so wrong," said Hannah.

The butch was in her face now. "What? You saying she's wrong?"

"No," said Hannah. "It's wrong that the League stayed white. I know all about that. I hate that about it. I wish it were a different story. I *know* how good you are."

The elegant femme gasped at this last remark, and Hannah realized how it sounded. Several other bar patrons had spilled out by now, and Hannah's teammate had completely disappeared, running noisily back to the truck stop. She was alone.

Fedora woman had not moved an inch away from Hannah's sweaty face. "You don't know me from Adam. You looking for a beat down, you come to the right place. You looking for a beer, your money's no good here. You looking for a woman, you not welcome."

All of a sudden, Hannah knew why she was there. "No beat down, no beer, no woman unfortunately," she spoke as evenly as possible. "I'm just here for one hour, and now that's half gone. Me, I'm looking for your good curve ball, to pass along to girls who want to learn."

Gusts of laughter greeted this declaration, but the woman in the fedora narrowed her eyes. "You serious?"

"Pretty much," said Hannah, who had just realized who she was dealing with. "You're Pico Blue, aren't you? From the Negro League team. You got turned away from the all-white league and offered a spot playing with the Negro League men for one season when a couple of players were sent overseas. But the men won't let you pitch even though you have a better curve ball, because you're still a woman. I know about that. Well, I'm here to say I respect you. I tell kids about you. And I think I still have twenty minutes. Teach me everything you know."

Pico looked at her for a moment, considering, and then turned to her date. "Carlotta, get me my ball bag and glove. They're in the car."

"For real? We're supposed to be dancing!"

"Just do it," said Pico Blue, and Hannah thought, *There's a slogan someone waited to use in my time.*

They moved into the alley. Pico wound up, and Hannah was flat on her back in seconds, with the real lump on her head rising. *That's why she was called Lumpy! That's why she called it her piece of history! She couldn't tell anyone she'd gone to a dyke bar and practiced with black players! It was all forbidden; she would have been suspended! The AAGPBL thought she got the lump on her head from that game against the Daisies!*

"Sorry," said Pico. "You got to shift sideways to catch me. Or didn't your friends tell you I'm a southpaw?" She wound up again, and Hannah, who had improvised a bat out of an old broom leaning against the house, managed to avoid being beaned yet again by chipping wildly at the pitch. The ball clunked up over their heads and landed in the gutter.

"Shit," said Pico. "I'm not climbing up there in this suit. You go up there and get me my ball. Ladder's just beyond that back window."

Hannah moved unsteadily along the house wall. Through the back window she could see women in butch-femme finery caressing, drinking beer, dancing to jazz, kissing in deep arm-chairs. Someone was serving up bowls of food from a big iron stewpot. Hearts and stars made from painted cardboard were strung across the bar, spelling out the names of a couple cele-brating their anniversary. Ivy plants drooped from a high shelf. It looked startlingly like a night at Sappho's Bar and Grill—a place to go, to belong, to celebrate and kiss, eat comfort food and talk. This was the parallel world of segregation. This was separate and unequal, a site not written into the record of women's history—yet. We couldn't even go into each other's bars, Hannah thought. But could anyone in the backroads of Grand Rapids in 1945 guess that thirty-one years into the future, the largest lesbian festival in the world would set up on a spot less than two hours' drive from there? With black and white les-bians boldly out and proud onstage?

"Are you getting that ball?" shouted Pico. "I got a lady waiting on me."

Hannah could not take her eyes from the window. What was the name of this Michigan bar?

"Are you getting that ball?" the voice came again. And the voice grew higher. Then younger. "I got this lady waiting for me!"

Stupidly, Hannah looked at the baseball she was holding. It was Sunday afternoon on Willow Street. Two little girls, one black, one white, were standing in the front yard up the road and calling to her. Hannah felt her head: no bumps. Just her own springy Jewish hair. She was back in her own body, her own time!

She walked out of Willow Street, which would never again haunt her as it had. There were bigger ghosts to serve. "Here you go," she tossed the ball to Cubby. "But who's the lady waiting for you?"

"Miss Angie, my coach," the kid replied. "We've got practice up at school in an hour."

"For the new girls' baseball team," Susie explained. "Cubby's the pitcher! And coach is putting her in against the boys next weekend!"

"Miss Angie taught me a mean curve ball," Cubby admitted.

If she ever really needed a stiff drink at Sappho's, it was now. Hannah burst into the club just as Denise, Elaine, Vera, Mandy, and Jo were cheering the Yankees game. Bets had obviously been placed. Isabel was putting silver trays of snacks in front of everyone as they gathered under the new big-screen TV, and wads of cash shifted discreetly between trays.

"Elaine, Denise, I just met your kid," Hannah announced. "Nice little redhead. And her friend Cubby."

"Oh, Cubby's fantastic," Elaine confirmed. "We set her up with a personal trainer, Angela, the new athletic director just hired on campus. You know Angela's aunt once pitched in the Negro Leagues? Her nickname was Paco or Pico or something. Cubby's going to be just like her, maybe a pro someday!"

Hannah had put down a five-dollar bill for a beer. Isabel brought and uncapped the beer, then pushed some coins and a small bowl of Cracker Jack toward Hannah. It wasn't until she had taken four good swallows, and removed her eyes from the TV screen, that Hannah saw what was mixed in with her change: a tiny silver baseball glove, Maud Nora's Cracker Jack prize from 1945. She vaguely recalled it falling out of her uniform skirt pocket as she stood on tiptoe to peek into the window of the black lesbian bar in Grand Rapids. How had it ended up at Sappho's?

She looked at Isabel, who smiled back at her over the coins, saying quietly, "Yes, this is your change, the little change you asked for," and then went back to wiping down the bar.

Chapter Nine
Halloween

The morning of October 31st found Hannah standing at her splintered podium in classroom B-12, giving her standard "scary" Halloween lecture: a grim hour she nonetheless enjoyed, observing its impact on those students new to women's history. Dressed in her conical witch's hat over academic robes, she brandished what she hoped looked like a giant labrys (probably intended to be a medieval axe, and, like the hat, left over from last year's discount Halloween sale.) Dimming the overhead lights, Hannah began with the reminder that once upon a time this holiday was called Samhain, a part of the annual calendar in pagan Europe. With the coming of Christianity and religious orthodoxy, such practices began to be banned as devil worship and heresy, and a not incidental consequence was the Inquisition torture directed at midwives, whose wisdom and "potions" raised heretical alarm. Midwives, elders, the unmarried spinster who supported herself as an abortionist, all burned at the stake, millions of women and children. Some, Hannah added, were charged merely because they bore marks of physical difference: moles, an extra finger, and superfluous nipples called "witches' teats." "My grandmother Ruthie, herself, was born with *six* nipples," Hannah informed her shaken audience of first-years and sophomores, all of whom had shown up to class in commercial holiday outfits, the costumes of familiar female archetypes: princess, nun, call girl, bar wench, witch. "Witches' teats are more common than you think." Her eye fell on one student, dressed as a perfect Snow White, who flinched and shook her head: *Not me!*

The projector flared on, screening the film Hannah saved for Halloween every year: *The Burning Times*. Onscreen, medieval artists' paintings of peasant women being burned alive as witches alternated with actual photographs of torture implements from European museums. Stocks. Pillories. The iron maiden. The rack. Thumbscrews. Two students in different rows rose from their seats and, gagging, ran out of the lecture hall.

"Most of their names are lost to us now," Hannah added as the soundtrack faded slowly and the regular classroom lights flickered on. "We can remember these from New England. Anne Hutchinson, burned in the colonies. Elizabeth 'Goody' Knapp, hanged from a tree in Bridgeport, Connecticut, in 1653, charged with having witches' teats."

"My great-great-something grandmother," a student chimed in. "In *Texas.*"

"Some of my relatives in Scotland," a male student added.

"It's going on right now in some African villages. And, you know, before I came here I was home-schooled as a kid, because my parents didn't want me experiencing Halloween parties at the local elementary school, where I might be exposed to devil worship in class," said the head of the Feminist Student Union.

"Who is the scariest figure in our time? Is it still a witch?" Hannah asked the class. "Have we overcome our fear of the dark, at last? Or do we yet fear the witches amongst us?"

Silence. Then: "It's middle-aged radical feminists," a voice in the back contributed. "The scary women today are like you."

She was still thinking about that comment hours later as the sun went down in a flaming orange slice.

Hannah's plans for the evening included, first, helping to decorate Sappho's Bar for the big Halloween party, then taking Cubby and Susie trick-or-treating while their moms partied at the bar, and later returning herself for a nightcap with Isabel and the gang. She left a large plastic pumpkin filled with candy on her front stoop, hoping the first trick-or-treaters wouldn't take all of it, and then stepped off her porch with her witch robes swirling jauntily. Autumn dusk and leaf and wood smoke scent. The days were shorter now, the evening a last luxury of warm, lingering light. The moon would rise later, a round, portentous globe, and the whole of the night lay ahead in haunted mystery.

Everything felt like a treat. But now it was time to pull her annual trick. Hannah's first task was the mild mischief of putting a hex on someone, and this year that meant leaving a rotten egg in the driveway of the town's most notorious homophobe, a man whose perpetual letters to the editor demanded the death penalty for "sodomites." No lights were on at his well-known house, and Hannah swiftly crouched to tuck the foul eggs under his parked car wheel, avoiding eye contact with bumper stickers that snarled ADAM AND EVE, NOT ADAM AND STEVE and IF YOU CAN READ THIS, THANK THE DOCTOR WHO DIDN'T ABORT YOU. Had anyone seen her? Was she being watched? Not yet. Time to cover the front bumper of his Buick with a sticker of her own, WITCHES HEAL. She ran back to the sidewalk and lowered her eyes, smiling.

Shadows gathered and moved across the street—halfway to darkness now, but the fading light still liquid enough to outline fresh Halloween decorations on porches. This block, Garfield Street, was one long swish of magic broom décor, with porch ghosts and animatronic spiders and laugh boxes and black cats aplenty, and the famous "haunted house" she knew Cubby and Susie would beg to visit. Bagged entirely inside a billowing sack—probably rented from Hannah's one-night-stand Flick, the pest control contractor—this house resembled a giant head with an open, screaming mouth for a doorway, barely covered by a thin flap of cheesecloth each child had to pass through for treats. The *vagina dentata*, thought Hannah, hurrying to get to Sappho's on foot and on time, but inexorably drawn to the warmly lit houses she passed by.

She wasn't a twenty-something any more. Neither child nor parent, just a dangerous ghost, a remnant of lesbian feminism, here to haunt everyone with her theories of women's history and her scolding about honoring the past. Well, the autumn and the night in her own life were fast approaching and her own house was dark. No lover, no partner kept that home fire burning as she wandered out in search of a social life tonight. Hannah scuffed through leaves and twigs and pods, gazing into other peoples' households, all so tenderly normal in appearance despite the macabre outerwear of pumpkin light and phony webs and skulls. Framed in basement kitchen windows, newlywed yuppies chopped vegetables on Ikea cutting boards, mixed martinis in blenders.

I am haunted by every woman I have ever loved. I am haunted by Gail, the one ex who won't talk to me. Isn't there a word for that, when they act like you're dead to them? Yes, and it's called ghosting. Wasn't she supposed to be settled, married, partnered by now? Had she blown it? Would she sail through the rest of her adult life like a leaf skittering over sidewalk, examining lives of the past while her own went undeveloped? Who was waiting for Hannah with a martini?

Well, Isabel was. Isabel had always been there. Maybe . . . could it be that Isabel was the one Hannah had been waiting for?

The inside of Sappho's was an orange nightmare. Candy corn had spilled from a bucket and was sticky underfoot, and crepe paper flecked with toy spiders dangled from every bar stool. "Boooo," Hannah howled cheerfully as she entered, scaring nobody.

"It's Doc! We're just about to—HACHOO!" Letty sneezed in greeting, jabbing a resentful thumb at the simmering smoke from Isabel's pot of brew. The scent was not unpleasant, but its smoky haze tickled even Hannah's nose. "Sorry, Letty," Isabel called, hastening from behind the bar to contain the spreading fumes. With a practiced flick of her wrist she slid a heavy lid over the stewpot. Immediately, the smoke disappeared. The scent changed to fresh-baked pastry, redolent of cloves. Now both Hannah and Letty found their mouths watering instead of their eyes.

"She's a witch," Letty nodded toward Isabel, not without admiration, and Hannah thought, *I am starting to arrive at that conclusion myself.* But Isabel was summoning everyone: "It's ready now." And they gathered around the cauldron, where Isabel had set out thirteen shot glasses embossed with a spiderweb pattern. Each woman took a glass, and carefully Isabel ladled out a bit of the pastry-scented liqueur. Dressed as ghosts, as Pacific Northwest saloon madams, furry rabbits, satanic rock stars and Star Trek characters, the regulars and old-timers of Sappho's Bar and Grill raised their glasses high and looked expectantly toward Isabel. But Isabel nudged Hannah.

"Oh. Right," Hannah fumbled. "Well, then. A toast. 'Round about the cauldron go,'" she quoted Shakespeare. She cleared her throat and closed her eyes.

"Once again we gather on a night known in the past as a women's holiday. Even as we dress in mock witch clothing, we remember.

"We remember the Salem witch trials. The accused children locked in Puritan prisons by well-fed magistrates. Ursula Kemp, hanged in England in 1582 for curing. Susanna Edwards, who probably suffered from Parkinson's disease, charged as a witch and executed in 1683. The widow Katharina Kepler, accused by neighbors of turning herself into a cat in 1611 in Germany. We remember all those who were tortured to confess until the Witchcraft Act of 1735.

"We drink sweetness to these women charged as witches, the known and unnamed nine million. The victims of the purges. The midwives, the warlock men called *faggots,* the elders mocked as *grannies.* Witches, healers, rise and fly tonight." They all sipped in unison. Hannah heard Letty swallow and gasp, *"Damn."* The liqueur burned her throat, too, in a strangely stimulating way. She felt, rather than thought, that if she spoke now it would be in a foreign language. And just at that moment, a woman screamed.

"Shit!" Moira spit out her mouthful of brew, soaking the front of her Irish banshee costume.

"It's just me—I'm so sorry—I saw those spiders, and then I realized they're fake! They're all fake," Denise apologized. She and her partner, Elaine, dressed as bowling balls, filled the doorway, their roundly costumed bodies partially blocking two nine-year-olds from heading further into the bar. Susie and Cubby peeked around Elaine's legs and waved at Hannah. "It's her, that lady who got our baseball," Cubby announced.

"That's no lady; that's Dr. Stern," Elaine laughed. "She's going to take the two of you trick-or-treating on Garfield Street."

"YEAH!" the girls rejoiced. "Can we go to the spook house that looks like a giant head? And the one that's haunted? And the one with the crazy woman who gives out silver money?"

"Do not go to any door without Hannah, and let her look over any treats handed to you," ordered Denise, plopping her bowling-body onto a barstool and waving a ten-dollar bill for a Halloween beer. Then she noticed the circle of women standing solemnly around Isabel's chef cauldron. "Oh. Right. The witch thing."

"Sorry," added Elaine. "We stepped in it again. We're never on time, and we're never politically correct." Then she pulled her hand from the doorjamb, startled. "I know that's a fake spider, but . . . it bit me!"

The mood broken, Hannah threw back the rest of her tribute cup and wiped her mouth on a party napkin. "Come on, kids. One hour. I'll walk you back through time, and guard your candy."

The sober rituals of history now gave way to the sheer fun Hannah remembered from her own 1960s childhood: time to hit up houses for chocolate caramels. She clutched Susie and Cubby's sweaty palms firmly in her own as they wound away from Sappho's and back to the start of the suburbs, on foot through temporarily blocked-off streets. The years peeled off Hannah like curls of lemon zest as they scurried, giggling, into the melee of the town's most beloved trick-or-treating strip. Monsters, firefighters and baby ballerinas fought for position in front of the haunted house, each child trembling, then determinedly moving forward into the grotesquely chortling "mouth." A public address system blasted forth howls of doom as the cheesecloth door flapped, but every kid came out earning, triumphant, clutching a bag of candy. Puddles of brightly wrapped bars littered the lawn. Hannah bent down and inspected a fresh, unwrapped packet dropped by some fleeing child.

"Mallo Cups! I haven't seen those since I was twelve," Hannah marveled.

"I've never seen them at all," Susie shuddered. "They look gross. I like 'Nerds.'"

"You would," Cubby shoved her.

Hannah shoved both of them to the front of the line, then leaned back against a parked car, enjoying the scene before her. Costumed college students lurched by in packs, already drunk. A few police officers were keeping an eye on things, shaking their heads at a pack of fraternity pledges costumed in blackface. Hannah thought about confronting and educating these frat brothers. Two were obviously her own students, recognizable by their high-top sneakers. Just then a fundamentalist preacher approached several young trick-or-treaters, brandishing anti-Halloween literature. The garishly illustrated pamphlets showed Satan pulling the puppet strings of innocent kids, and wealthy homosexuals falling into the flaming pits of hell. "Thanks, I'll take those!" she snarled, shoving the literature into her backpack pocket for later shredding. "We hope to clean up this decadent devil holiday," the evangelist told her, and Hannah responded "So do I!," whisking out her toy witch broom and sweeping the sidewalk with it, much to the delight of three gay men dressed as Fruit Loops.

"Read your palm, darling?" called the fortuneteller, whose real origins were unknown but who sat in the same cane-bottomed chair at the same corner every Halloween, speaking only to women. Hannah pulled out a five-dollar bill and opened her hand. But as she scrutinized the palm before her, the fortune-teller's all-knowing eyes widened and then shut. *"What in the world?"* she groaned, shoving Hannah's money into her ample cleavage, then shaking her head. "I can't tell you what I'm seeing here, darling, for you would not believe it and they would arrest me for lying," she whispered. "So please—how about, maybe, just a handwriting analysis?"

Wondering what fresh madness lay in store for her, predictable only by a palm reader who now refused to divulge any informa-tion, Hannah sighed and wrote out her name on a candy wrapper. Then she blinked.

"You see," the fortuneteller murmured.

It was Hannah's handwriting, all right. But not the cursive script that she used now. Her name had somehow turned into the block letters of her second-grade signature—the way she might have written her name as a child out trick-or-treating. All of a sudden she remembered school penmanship lessons. It had been easy and fun for her to learn to write her name, as *Hannah* was exactly the same whether written backwards or forwards.

"You are that person who goes backwards and forwards," said the fortuneteller, reading her mind as well as her palm, then picking up her chair and running from Hannah, who was left to stand there in confusion, looking at her name on a Mallo Cup wrapper.

Susie materialized at Hannah's side, drooling chocolate from a mouthful of Raisinettes. "Hey, how come people tortured witches long ago?" she asked. "We heard you. At the club."

"What kind of torture?" Cubby demanded. "Like what they did to black people in slavery times?"

Oh, man, thought Hannah. There is nowhere to turn without hitting the great historical wall of human suffering built here on

122

planet Earth. How do I break it down for nine-year-olds tonight? Cubby was watching her. "The church leaders thought witches were women who used too much power, in a time when only the Christian priests were allowed to have power," she offered. "Old women who seemed too smart, too good at healing, scared the new believers. And Cubby, you're right that slavery was torture. The way that women were tortured when someone accused them of witchcraft was different. It involved tools we thankfully don't use today. I don't know how much you need to know. Okay, stretching people on a rack. Hurting their fingers with harsh pinchers called thumb screws."

"Gross!" Susie was fascinated.

Hannah was just about to pat herself on the back for her PG-rated version of *The Burning Times* when, unexpectedly, Cubby started to cry. "My fingers, my fingers," she wept.

"That scared you? It scares me, too," Hannah apologized, hugging her close. "Because I'm a writer. The thumbscrews always scared me most." She thought briefly of a night she'd spent in handcuffs, long ago when she was twenty-three, after a nonviolent sit-in and peace protest at a nuclear missile plant. She'd gone to jail for ten hours with four friends from her antiwar group, and during those long hours, left in a cell in the new plastic handcuffs used on the demonstrators, her hands had gone completely numb. She remembered the terror when she could no longer feel her own fingers. "And of course, Cubby, you have these extra magic hands to protect—you're a pitcher. Look, no one's going to hurt your hands like that. I promise."

"But they could. I had my arm broken in second grade by a bully. He teased me all year because I was smarter and bigger and I pitched better than him. Plus he said stuff like I'm black, I don't have a mom, my best friend has two moms so I must be a queer too. He called me every bad word I'm not allowed to say. *Coon. Lesbo.* The n-word. He broke my arm, and I had to wear a sling and miss six weeks of practice. They made him go to that special school, but I hear he shoved another girl there. Then *she* got her fingers hurt." Cubby sniffled. Susie stood on one foot and then the other, embarrassed, rustling through her pumpkin bag full of treats for something soothing. "Here." She offered Cubby a Powerhouse bar. "Because you're my friend. *You're a powerhouse!*"

What in the hell? Hannah thought. *First Mallo Cups, now a Powerhouse bar? This stuff isn't made anymore. You can't get these around here—unless someone's been hoarding retro candy bars just to hand them out at Halloween. Unless . . .* She hugged the two girls again for a long minute, and they moved on.

And the parked cars changed. The license plates showed earlier years. At the next house, they received more time-warp treats. Cubby and Susie screamed "TRICK OR TREAT" and a tanned arm dropped Milkshake and Butternut bars into their bags. Two doors down, the take included Clark bars, Zagnuts, Sugar Mamas, Marathon Bars. At the next houses the girls collected Brach's Chocolate Stars, Charms, Beeman's Teaberry gum, Turkish Taffy, and wax bottles, as Hannah's teeth started to chatter. They were heading farther back in time at every house on Garfield Street. "Is this crack?" Cubby asked anxiously, holding out a crystallized gob of rock candy.

"You guys almost ready to go?" Hannah barked, feeling the mist of spookdom rising in her chest. "Got enough candy?" Other children around her were probing the contents of their Halloween buckets with similar confusion.

"Are you kidding? We still haven't been to the crazy woman's house!" shouted Cubby, who had apparently forgotten all about witches, torture, and schoolyard backlash and, along with Susie, was now riding high on sugary time-travel candy bars. "Check this out—black candy!" She offered Hannah a selection from her bag: indeed, Black Cow bars, Blackjack gum. They approached the bent fencing of a home everyone usually avoided: the residence of town eccentric Misty Romanoff, an elder who wore her old figure-skating outfit and pancake makeup to the Safeway. Both warmhearted and harmless, she really did give out money on Halloween. One year, greeting a little girl at the door who also hoped to become a champion skater, she had given away her

Olympic medal. Children were lined up three deep on her front walk, watched by anxious parents.

As Cubby and Susie took their places in line for silver dollars, Hannah watched sugar-wired children fight over candy, trade, boast, jostle, and throw up. Two girls were fighting over a candy necklace that definitely looked vintage 1950s. Another child had retreated from the fray and was playing hopscotch by herself, solemnly adorable in a 1920s sailor suit costume. She gave a grunt of exasperation as she tossed her hopscotch marker and it rolled toward the curb. As Hannah bent down and rescued it from the gutter, their eyes met, and the old framed photo on Hannah's living room mantel sprang to life. This little girl was Hannah's grandmother, the one born with six nipples. Witches teats. Ruthie.

Somewhere behind them, a front door banged and Susie and Cubby raced toward Hannah, panting, waving their hands. "We got silver dollars!" they shouted. "Can we go now?" Then they stopped, for Hannah was talking to someone. Someone they could not see.

Stuffed with old-time candy, the girls were safely back at Sappho's by nine p.m., and Hannah stayed for a quick drink and a game of pool. Yet she felt a strange depression she could not name. Perhaps it was the annual return to the topic of witch persecution, expanded upon by the evening's reminders of racist bullying and homophobia. So much to confront. So much that a feminist historian could never forget. What she really wanted was simply to be at home, by herself, eating those mystically apparitional Mallo Cups and watching *Dracula's Daughter*. She bade everyone a Happy Halloween and walked home, looping through neighborhoods still bristling with costumed children.

Thumbscrews. Handcuffs. How had she held up under torture? Badly. She thought back to that night in the holding cell, absurdly arrested for peace, a threat to nobody, yet shackled for "criminal trespass." All of them, the women in her peace brigade, were kept in tight plastic handcuffs overnight until their release

125

(charges dropped) at dawn. Through that night her fingers swelled, her hands went numb, and cold sweat trickled between her breasts as she pondered the possibility of real nerve damage. What if she never wrote again? Could she survive and complete grad school? How would she type her dissertation? Her nose itched; her hands were cuffed behind her back. She'd leaned her head against Isabel's chest for one moment just to scratch her nose on a shirt button. A tall security officer shouted "None of that, dykes," and had them separated. Hannah was dragged roughly to a different cell, her shoulder nearly dislocated. Because they were pacifists. Because they were lesbians. Because they were feminists. Because they were—

Witches, hissed a voice. *Like your granny. Driven from the Old Country, wasn't she? And good riddance. Show us if ye have the witch marks too. Unbind thy breasts.*

Hannah whirled around; no one was there. Then, to her horror, she felt unseen hands start to unhook her teaching bra. She dropped to the ground and rolled into the protective fetal position she recalled from the old days of nonviolent demonstrations. *Civil disobedience.* "I disobey you!" she shouted in the empty, dark street. The bra flapped limp against her cold shoulder blades. No one was there.

Then Hannah stood alone, and flashed her breasts upward, toward the tree branches where she heard the faintest hissing whispers fading, fading. "If normal tits, still a wild witch at heart," she whispered, wiggling all ten fingers. "No thumbscrews on these hands tonight. I write the witches into history."

When Hannah arrived home thirteen blocks later, her front porch still held a bucket of candy, but not the treats she'd left for the neighborhood kids earlier. These were candy brands that had not been manufactured for fifty years or more, with a stick of half-used hopscotch chalk across the top. She brought it all in, put it on the coffee table, turned on her movie, and laid her conical hat next to her old landline phone. The answering machine was blinking furiously, with the first three messages from graduate students wishing her a happy Halloween but in actuality wanting her notes on their dissertation chapters. It wasn't until she turned down the TV volume to hear the very quiet fourth message that she recognized the voice: her own dead father, saying "Well. Hello." It wouldn't play again, though she sat there, wide-eyed, pushing and pushing REPLAY until dawn.

Chapter Ten
Thanksgiving

That November was memorable for its day after day of glorious autumn leaf and swirl, blazing leaves first limp and then crisp underfoot, leaves that caught under her windshield wipers, in her backpack straps, her bicycle gears and wheel spokes, even in her mailbox. The insistent whisper and whisk and scratch and crunch of ever more beautiful hand-shaped leaves began to feel to Hannah like letters, sent express mail to her on rare winds from somewhere, tugging, insistent. *Look at me. Pay attention. What about me? Me, too. Am I not as beautiful? Soon I will fade. Don't you want to collect me, too?* But were these spirits the spirits of her own students, who, now peaking in their attachment to what she taught, would soon enough leave the tree of learning and graduate into a still-unfeminist world? Or were these leaves the spirits of women past, the women she taught about—perhaps some she had skipped, failed to mention altogether? To how many, exactly, did she owe allegiance?

Best not to think about it too much, Hannah mused in leaf-kicking pleasure, running through piles of mulch and acorns like a kid. I'll think about it later, she told herself as sunlight on hayfields tempted her to visit country farm markets each Saturday in November. She'd come home at day's end with her Women and Children First Bookshop bag bulging with local honey, cherry jam, cinnamon cider, turnips, parsnips, syrup, arugula, yellow carrots, beets. The rising passion in her heart on such outings was for root vegetables, not for women, or one particular woman, or the arc of women's history. Something in her Jewish genes always stirred, just before Thanksgiving, remembering life in the Old Country. There, forbidden to own land, Jews did the best they could with kitchen gardens and root cellars, emerging not only with sturdy foods for soups but with an entire enraged language of Yiddish curses based around root vegetables. These curses had always helped Hannah cheerfully negotiate the perpetual small annoyances of academic life: "Beets should grow from your belly!" she shrieked at the university garage employee who ticketed her car despite its clearly displayed parking permit. "*Zol vaksen tsibiles fond a pupik*—May onions sprout from your navel!" she hurled at the broken copy machine. It was late autumn, the roadside stands beckoned with pre-Thanksgiving produce, the leaves stuck to her sleeves, and she couldn't get anything done. She was foraging, devouring, packing on the calories for winter when, bear-like, the urge to feast would fade. In a month, she would crave only hibernation and sleep—just as final exam time struck. For now, she couldn't keep her backside in a chair to read a book, not with leaf-mapped trails calling to her bike.

The last class before Thanksgiving vacation, though, was one of her absolute favorites, listed on her women's history syllabus as "The Fun Food Lecture." Half of her students had already left early, skipping Tuesday classes for better airfares and train fares home, the first-year students exploding with homesickness and new knowledge, ready to confront their anxious, tuition-paying parents over the turkey: *Mom! Dad! I've become a feminist. My women's history professor says...* Hannah had begged them, "Don't make me the bad guy! Don't ruin the dinner with your big provocative announcement of how radical you are now. Let everyone eat. Let your families enjoy having you home for a day before you let them have it with your new college persona. If you're serious about identifying with feminism, bear in mind how hard the *women in your family* probably worked to get that Thanksgiving dinner together while you were comfortably reading your Jewelle Gomez vampire novel on the train homeward." But in spite of her advice, every year a few of her favorite new students stood up just before dinner was served and, gripping a great-grandmother's lace-knit tablecloth, declared "I won't eat your filthy turkey any more, Mother—I'm a vegan now." Or: "I've joined the Socialist Workers." "I'm transitioning: Call me Eddie, not Edna." "Mom and Dad, I'm leaving the Church to become a Buddhist nun." "This is my new boyfriend and, yes, he's a Muslim. We're engaged! Did I mention I'm pregnant?"

Today, the students who had not yet departed for airports and family drama filed into the lecture hall, lighthearted at having made it this far through the semesters, beaming as they awaited the "fun" lecture that came before Thanksgiving. Hannah stood at the chalkboard, smiling back at them. "I know that many of you," she began, "are itching to get home to your families, and for most of you that means a traditional Thanksgiving meal, and the ritual foods you long for with nostalgia. Okay, you've just had ten weeks of women's history. Let me ask: What's *gendered* about this holiday meal?"

They all burst out laughing. "OMG, it's the most gendered holiday *ever,*" nodded Molly. "It's total hunting and gathering, in a way. I mean, let's face it! The women do all the vegetables and cooking and mashing and serving, and the men just carve the meat."

"Or tend the bar and watch football," a male student added. "My dad sometimes grills kebabs, though; we're Lebanese."

"The men use what look like weapons—carving tools—or they do food prep that's outside, like Ali said," Janice contributed. "The grill is outside, the barbecue pit is outside, the men play touch football outside. The women are inside using more harvest-y type tools."

131

"You're all over eighteen," Hannah pointed out. "In just a few years you'll be setting up your own households. How many of you feel ready to carry on the traditional Thanksgiving meal yourselves with the families you'll create? Janice? Molly? Keisha? Any of you feel ready to prepare and serve a full Thanksgiving dinner to your guests?"

Gasps of horror greeted her inquiry. "Hell, no," Molly shook her pink-dyed head. "I can about boil water. I don't know any of those recipes."

"We eat dorm food," Ali reminded Hannah. "I mean, some guys live off-campus or in the frats, but most of us pay up to use the dining hall during our four years here. We don't get many chances to learn basic food prep unless we take summer jobs in restaurants. My mom is always trying to show me how to select a ripe avocado or a melon. It's a mystery to me."

"And, like, that info just isn't passed down from mother to daughter as much anymore, if that's what you're looking for," said Janice, who was always eager to provide the "right" answer in class. "Maybe our mothers took home ec in high school, but we didn't have to. We all took computer programming. We grew up zapping snacks in a microwave or eating fast food on weekends."

"Yeah, it's not like I ever saw a cow, growing up in Brooklyn," Keisha explained. "I had no idea where butter came from. They sent me to Fresh Air Fund camp and I had to collect eggs, and sometimes they were not only warm but covered in chicken poo! It freaked me out. But in Africa, lots of girls still live traditionally, agriculturally and all."

"Any one of you grow up on an actual working farm?" Hannah asked. Not a single arm was raised. She turned to the board.

"Okay, let's start with all the skills we have lost. In pre-industrial Europe, in colonial America, any girl who wasn't born into an elite family had to learn the basics for running her own household one day by age ten. She could be married off or sent into servitude at ten, eleven. How did her typical day start?" Her hand moved rapidly up and down as they made the enormous list.

In the dark. She'd rise before dark to the crowing of roosters—no clock, no watch, no alarm bell. Before starting breakfast she'd have to get firewood, walk with its weight and break it or chop it herself. Get a fire going, then fetch the water, and if there's no well on her land that's another long walk to the river, the town well, the spring, or the creek. That's when stranger danger begins. The strange man in those woods.

"What's in breakfast?" Hannah asked, and they called out "Eggs. You have to collect eggs." "Butter. You have to be able to milk a cow and churn butter, and make cheese . . . and make bread. Women knew how to grow wheat and rye and flax and corn, how to make flour, bake bread in an oven." Hannah interrupted, "Yes, good, but we all come from different traditions, here. What are the breads of your foremothers?"

Now they were hungry and longing for the taste of home, of heritage, of ethnic pride and comfort food and love. Everyone yelled at once. *Challah. Chapati. Kolache. Biscuits and cornbread. Panini. Irish soda bread. Bean paste bun. Fry bread. Tortilla. Crepe. Lavash. Beignets. Pita. Shoofly pie. Babka.*

"Can any of you make those foods? Will those traditions continue with you?"

Silence. Heads hung. "I know how to make brownies," boasted Francesca, and after a moment she conceded, "But my grandmother's homemade pasta; that tradition will probably end with her. I mean, I buy my noodles at the corner store!"

"This exercise isn't meant to make you feel guilty; and I know how you feel," Hannah assured them. "My own grandmother grew up with a live carp swimming around in her bathtub every Friday to make gefilte fish. I certainly haven't carried on that skill, although I inherited a love of gefilte fish if somebody else makes it."

"Ewwwwwww," from the non-Jewish students.

They returned to the Skills of Our Foremothers list on the board. Young farm girls, preparing for marriage, once knew every aspect of cooking, growing and preparing food, making clothing, tending animals, predicting weather, protecting and pruning orchards, vegetable gardens, herbal medicine gardens. The lists filled the first chalkboard and spilled over onto the spare rolling chalkboard behind the lecture hall stage. *Planting rice. Plowing. Winnowing. Haymaking. Chopping cotton. Preserving jelly. Boiling. Frying. Rendering fat. Roasting, Deglazing. Churning. Poaching. Koshering. Baking. Simmering. Weaving. Spinning. Carding wool. Sewing. Knitting. Quilting, Embroidering. Knitting. Dyeing. Making candles, soap, baskets, pottery, cradles, tablecloths, lace . . .*

"I can't do any of these things," Hannah confessed. "I am a different kind of woman. Nor did I marry, or have children. In the past, I'd be a 'spinster', but that's based on the idea I could spin. I do make a mean mashed turnip dish, though. Now scoot!"

They headed out of the classroom, talking agitatedly, pausing to wish her a happy Thanksgiving. "God," Hannah overheard two students say, "I'm going to get my great-aunt's recipes right now! I'm going to learn how to make brisket if it kills me! I'm going to take a class in quilting; and make jam . . ."

I didn't learn any of those things. I teach a history of domestic life I never lived myself. What do I know how to do, anyway, except teach? Will the material legacy of women's culture die with me?

The wet weekend came at the end of Thanksgiving vacation. Hannah felt the storm even before she heard rain with her ears, waking to a drenching, rocking rain on that last Saturday in November, just after she'd gone home to her mother's for the holiday (*beets, potatoes and carrots, oy vay!*) and then returned to catch up on lost work time. Her first thought was gratitude: At last, a wet day for staying at home to get things done. A return to immersion in women's history. But then she remembered the annual Thanksgiving gathering at Sappho's was later that afternoon. She'd have to make use of the morning, cooking—and hopefully the storm wouldn't deter too many guests from driving in to the bar for their beloved holiday event.

Peeling turnips for the buttered mashed dish she was supposed to bring over for Isabel's feast, Hannah looked affectionately at her snug apartment. Rain and history might shake her rafters, but her books and papers kept her anchored in her chosen life's work.

134

As her hands scraped and chopped, she could sense the multitudes, the eons of women before her who had engaged in this simple work of feeding others—mothers, daughters, servants, apprentices. Her eye fell on the book left open on her rocking chair: Alice Clark's *Working Life of Women in the Seventeenth Century*. Then, just as she turned back to her wooden cutting board, for an instant she saw an unfamiliar rough sleeve extending down her wrist—not the pilled cotton of her Berkshire Conference of Women's History sweatshirt but a scullery maid's leg-of-mutton sleeve. Scared, she backed away from the stove, and her apron fluttered, an apron she did not own, had never worn. The apron strings tied to someone else's life.

Abruptly she was herself again, in her women's basketball sweatpants, Ugg boots and her beet-stained feminist history conference pullover. The turnips began to simmer in the pot. And adrenaline simmered in her bloodstream. She paced. The apartment was shaking from storm winds now. And Hannah was shaking, again, from the past reaching out to her with its crone-like fingers. Touching her.

The phone rang and the lights went out at the exact same time. Hannah stumbled over a turnip that had somehow rolled underfoot, banged her ankle hard against the counter edge, and grabbed for the phone in the sudden darkness, for one second expecting the voice to be a sad servant-girl from colonial America. But it was only Isabel. "Hi! Are you still planning to join us tonight?"

"Of course I am. I'm making the *fucking turnips* right now," Hannah growled, relieved and bruised, rubbing her ankle. "Are you getting slammed by this rain? I just lost the power here, except for some reason the telephone works." The lights flickered back on.

"It's fine over here. There are about six women already at the bar, cooking," Isabel responded, sounding amused. "If we lose power at the bar, we'll use Jo's camp stoves to reheat the dishes— she brought four of them. I'm just checking in with everyone so we know how much to make. Trale's bringing goulash, no matter what. Looks like a number of women may have their driveways flooded by afternoon. But we have at least twenty coming, plus we're counting on you." Isabel paused. "And your turnips!" She laughed and hung up.

Hannah sat down, staring at her hands.

We're counting on you. Well, she was a beloved member of her own community, that much was certain. And it was Thanksgiving, a week of renewed gratitude for what they shared at Sappho's. But, glancing again at her textbooks on colonial women's history, Hannah wondered what in fact she herself could be counted on to do in her own time.

At four o'clock the rain was still pounding, loudly, and the leak in the window frame in Hannah's bedroom was dropping pings of tree-root-smelling water into the mop bucket positioned below. But the rest of her apartment was redolent of buttered and seasoned turnips, and Hannah decided to forgo body oil altogether as she toweled from a shower. Why disturb the Thanksgiving smell of food, nature, and warm womanhood? She pulled on nice wool pants, good boots, and a dark red cowl-neck sweater and walked carefully to her car, balancing umbrella, covered dish, keys. The entire neighborhood smelled like food, a medley of competing ovens, microwaves, wood stoves, and uncorked wines.

Yes, the roads were flooded in places, where broken branches and piled-up sopping leaves had blocked curbside drains. But other cars were out, negotiating delicately, with drivers in holiday moods of you-go-first kindness and solicitude. At the last stoplight before Sappho's Bar and Grill, five cars scrambled around two small harvest pumpkins that had blown off a closed produce stand and were now merrily rolling around the four-way traffic intersection. Hannah glanced at the dish strapped child-like into the passenger seat, but her own vegetables remained passive. She panicked briefly when she spotted a police cruiser in her rear-view mirror, blinking at her, then realized it was Officer Angie, also on her way to the bar for the holiday event.

Sappho's was festive in the best fashion. Sprays of perfect autumn leaves, their edges outlined in gold paint, decorated the walls, ceiling beams, bar posts and chair backs. The pool table was temporarily covered with a sheet of plywood and a golden-dyed cloth, and rows of dishes gleamed richly from ceramic and wooden bowls. One long table with extra folding chairs along each side was set with silverware and gourds, vases of flowers, and a very large punch bowl steaming with some sort of mulled cider. A stack of dried corn tied to a pouch of tobacco honored the indigenous Native Americans, starkly reminding those feasting of the vanished indigenous communities whose ways had sustained the lives of white colonists.

Hannah left her wet rain jacket in the hallway and entered smiling, leaving her mashed turnips on the pool table. Behind her, Officer Angie was peeling off a leather overcoat and, as Isabel's rules required, she entered without her weapon. "It's locked in the car," she assured Isabel, who welcomed her.

"You made it!" several voices called to the new arrivals. Other women, too, were scraping wet boots at the door and proffering hot food baskets. It might have been any Thanksgiving gathering scenario, thought Hannah, except for the absence of male guests and the very friendly kissing exchanged between women. In point of fact, Dog and Yvette's mouths had yet to separate. "Would you two stop making out and help me with this frickin-ass *bird?*" was Letty's rather un-Pilgrim like command, and other couples popped apart as well to finish setting the table and basting.

Trale, having finished tuning the bar's damp piano, began a quiet medley of "Simple Gifts" and "Amazing Grace" until Carol ordered her to offer "something more dykey," and then Moira shouted "I'm on it" and turned on the sound system, which Isabel had cued up with sexy food-themed blues tunes from the 1930s and '40s. Soon they were all standing arm in arm around the table.

"I guess this is where we ought to say grace," Yvette ventured, and Letty, hovering over both the basted bird and the sculpted tofu platter with an elegant serrated knife in each gnarled hand, sighed loudly, and paused in the middle of carving.

"What are you thankful for?"

Isabel had carefully poured a measure of amber-colored cider or mulled wine into everyone's cup before posing this question. Beautifully dressed, wrapped in a velvet cape, she smiled at her guests from her place at the head of the table. In response, faces beamed back at her—or went blank, according to personality.

"I'll start," Dog offered. "I am thankful I am not forced to observe this holiday with my homophobic mother and drunk father, and that I have a family here who built a space of love."

"Amen," from Yvette.

Tongues loosened. "I'm thankful that I found y'all when I was ... was pretty close to suicide," shared Emily. "I'm close to that B.A. because of all of you—and Dr. Stern, of course," she toasted her professor.

Hannah glowed with pleasure. "I'm thankful for you too. For all of the brave students who dare to take a *women's* history class."

"For those who came before us," added Trale. "Dykes of every decade, every class."

"I'm thankful for the motherline of feminism."

"Enough to eat, this year, for so many of us."

"My family who support me."

"My partner, sitting here beside me, in spite of my bad temper and my snoring."

"For all people who fight racism."

"My baby girl!"

"My guru."

"My new electric wheelchair."

"My cats, my AA group, my Taiko drumming class."

"Yes, but ..." Shoni spoke with difficulty. "I want to ask this question. Who would you be if you had lived in colonial America at that first Thanksgiving we learn about in school? I would be the 'savage,' invited but the Other, we all know." She touched the tower of corn in front of her.

While Letty carved and others helped serve, they all attacked this question, plates soon full—eating, drinking, interrupting, and laughing, then serious again. "*You*, my dear, would wear the scarlet letter," Janey poked her partner, Amy, with a fork.

"And I'd be hanged for bearing a mixed-race baby," Letty sighed. "I know about those old laws."

"Me, I'd be one of those indentured servant chicks," Emily announced through a mouthful of Brussels sprouts. "I'd leave behind a bad-girl personal history of having been a London brothel slut. I'd show up on a pier in Virginia, all demure in a frilly apron with a knife under my petticoat for any knave who tried to violate me during that long nauseous Atlantic crossing. I'd clean till I drop, faint, at the feet of my rich planter dude employer, then make him fall in love with me and marry me and will me his estate. Then we'd raise horses and I'd skip off to kiss the stable girl on weeknights, saving her the best cuts from the ham we'd had at supper."

"Jesus," from Moira. "No need to ask which of us took that class with Dr. Stern."

"You'd tire of being kept," said Trale. "You'd run away and join the Revolutionary War. I might pass as a man and play the music in those army camps. Be Deborah Sampson, but more of a yogi."

Hannah, already glutted on mashed potatoes and cornbread, was enjoying this, but had a question of her own. She accepted another glass of Isabel's mulled wine before she spoke. "Have you ever thought," she began, "about what it might have been like to leave England, or Northern Europe, or Spain during that whole long epoch of exploration and Crusading and piracy, in order to start a lesbian colony? A lesbian country, our own? I mean, as the Pilgrims and Puritans experimented with a community of their own. An escape from persecution, into autonomy."

"Well, forget that fantasy," Jeri put in. "The Pilgrims came in and settled their big, sanctimonious butts atop Shoni's people. There's no starting a utopian village anywhere on planet Earth without displacing whoever's already there."

"One group's refuge is another's land lost," said Shoni.

"Look at Israel and Palestine," someone else added.

"And no way to unite women across, you know, race and class and Protestant and Catholic, and language. Everyone distrusted and hated the next village, and women turned one another in to the Church or the law, happily letting someone else be tried as a witch. And it takes skills and training to run a colony, which women didn't get except as queens ruling from long distance. But there have been many attempts to create a utopian motherland in fiction, at least," Carol offered. "Look over there at Isabel's bar bookshelf. *Herland* was written in 1915! Then there's *Mists of Avalon, Daughters of a Coral Dawn, The Wanderground.*"

"If you want a lesbian autonomous community, what about that Oregon women's land collective? There's also that old directory of lesbian land communities over there on the bookshelf."

"I lived in one," Carol sighed. "And it was no utopia! My God, the arguments we had. I was nearly expelled for using the wrong kind of toothpaste. Then, after I had my son, I was out. The *processing . . .*"

"What about Michigan? The Michigan festival? Or any other women's music festival, you know? Those were lesbian mini-villages, for sure—all through the 1970s,'80s,'90s. There was processing and conflict at festivals, sure, but they were successful over time. Like annually reappearing cities of women. Lesbian colonies."

"And now mostly they're *gone,*" Dog hissed. "Disappearing. Like that Lost Colony."

"Like Brigadoon. Which appeared once every hundred years . . ."

"Look," Isabel interrupted suddenly. "Do play along here, for one minute—I believe that Hannah was imagining what a first *lesbian* Thanksgiving might have been like. Weren't you?"

"Well. Uh," Hannah sighed. "I, I picture a raggedy mothership of unwashed Amazons, landing not at Plymouth Rock but at P-town."

"Ha," from Trale.

"The question is who would be doing the cooking and serving at that original lesbian holiday, too. This is where feminist politics gets bogged down, you know. I mean, who cleans up? Who carves? Who sits where at the table? Who leads what kind of grace, and in what language?"

"We all share the work here at Sappho's, at our holiday meals," Moira pointed out. "No one person does all the labor. Well, of course Isabel does the drinks. But—"

"A recipe collection that shall never see print," Isabel smiled, pouring them all one more round. "Professional secrets."

"There's a caste system even in lesbian culture," said Carol. "Carpenters on top, child care workers below."

"That sounds about right—not to mention sexy," laughed Letty, as she reached for another helping of yams.

"I know that in a past life I might have been a servant, not a scholar," Hannah mused. "I wouldn't necessarily be the same kind of person I am now. I might have stripped the corn kernels, shelled the beans, plucked hen feathers, cleared away the corncobs at that first Thanksgiving, or at a later lesbian version."

"Good. Take these out to the compost heap now, my dear," Isabel directed, handing Hannah a platter of denuded corncobs. "Let's make some table space for the pies."

"PIES!" screamed everyone, forsaking any utopia but that of whipped cream heaped on pumpkin and pecan.

Hannah balanced the platter of corncobs, some trailing delicate fringes of corn silk, as she edged toward the back door of the bar. She could hear rain still pelting the roof, here where the eaves sloped thinly, and the lights were flickering again although that wasn't too much of an issue for the gathering now that most of the food had been cooked and served. With one foot she nudged open the back door, looking for the three garbage bins (one marked "COMPOST") that Isabel kept in the alley.

Rain smacked her in the face. The door banged shut. And in front of her was not the familiar, dumpster-lined alley, but a pier deck slick with salt crust, upon which women huddled, aprons pulled tight to their faces.

"Be you from the workhouse?"

It was a hoarse whisper. Hannah fell to the deck with a thump. The young woman next to her lowered the apron from her face slightly, just enough so that Hannah could see a tired eye surrounded by what could only be the lingering pockmarks of smallpox. "Don't ye puke, I'm over and through it," she added, pointing to her scars. "They sent me over to be indentured since no man will marry me now in London town. And you?"

"I'm at Thanksgiving dinner," was all Hannah could come up with.

"Bound over to serve the parson's house then. Well, you'll be fed, but mind ye his wandering hands!" The deck creaked suddenly with heavy feet. "The men come!"

"You? What can you bring a master?" asked a sneering agent. A child no more than ten obediently rose and then recited: "Card wool, mix dye, work a lye for soap. Wind thread, spin and knit, brew, make preserves, raise lambs, milk cows, churn, skim cream, set hens, stitch quilt patches, fix a lady's hair, mend gloves."

The woman next to Hannah, newly recovered from smallpox, extended her hands. "Look not upon me as a planter's wife but as an able chamber maid," she offered to a man who had stepped forward, hat pulled low.

"I look for a servant to do washing for my family of nine," he growled. "Wash and starch and iron and never mind thy two scarred hands."

Frantic, Hannah slipped back to the end of the long line of aproned women and tried to orient herself. *White women on a wet pier boasting their household skills.* This must be Thanksgiving week, after the time of the Pilgrims' first feast in 1621, but still colonial America. Sending over indentured female servants had not yet given way to sales of slaves. This pier wasn't yet an auction block. But what a sad-faced lot of women, children, teenagers with stretch marks of lost child-bearing, some women clearly dressed in prison garb marking them from Newgate back in England. There were any number of reasons for women to accept the unknown horrors of indenture if it paid passage across the ocean, putting them at good distance from the horrors they had come to know well. This was the *book* that Hannah taught each fall!

She always shivered when she came to that chapter assignment on indentured women:

Completely subject to the will of their masters or mistresses, they could neither leave nor marry until their time of service was up, and were severely punished if they tried to do so. Whippings were common, and brandings were inflicted for a second offense. Their terms were extended as punishment if they did marry, or if they bore an illegitimate child, even though this was often the master's son. Therefore they often resorted to child murder, even though the law required execution for this crime. No wonder that a servant woman in Virginia in 1623 wrote, "I thought no head had been able to hold so much water as hath and doth daily flow from mine eyes." *

Hannah knew what it meant to live in this era—not from personal experience but from hour after hour of poring over history's pages. Indentured servants were too often the most desperate women, released from crowded London jails and workhouses. Some had been prostitutes or were unmarried girls caught self-aborting, others shamed by rape at the hands of an upper-class master whose inherited status meant his victims could never see justice. In Scotland, local ballads passed these stories down as mournful melodies, depicting the plight of serving girls charged with infanticide. These and others headed to the New World colonies to redeem their souls through seven years of work. Their numbers grew with women banished by their families or former employers as well as those unable to pay fines for petty crimes, or unwelcome in poorhouses due to their sins. England's new "poor laws" could not sustain them with enough to eat, for while women did twice the work of men, they were allocated one-half the support. The disabled, anyone marked with difference, well, they didn't even rate charity, and instead were given caps and kicked into the streets to beg for coins, marked with the forever-lasting slur *handy-cap*. Maybe in the Massachusetts Colony, each could reinvent herself, but here they would encounter new oppressions in the religious laws bringing new and harsher punishments for such sins as running on a Sunday, gossip, and idleness. The stocks and dunking stool awaited them. And there was always, always the lurking possibility of being accused of witchcraft.

"Can ye wield a broom?" A man was prodding Hannah with his cane. She reacted instantly to the unwelcome sense of physical invasion, jumping up to standing posture and looking him in the eye. "I can ride one," she retorted.

He slapped her across the face. "We shan't suffer a witch!"

Several women then gathered protectively around Hannah, who touched her stinging cheek in astonishment. *No man has ever hit me.* One older woman reached up, pretending to straighten Hannah's dress collar, but as she did so tucked Hannah's star of David necklace out of sight under a fold of shawl. This woman leaned in and through rotting teeth whispered, "Jewess, hide thy worship. They have not yet built a temple here. Keep a hock of ham curing on thy rafter to quit inquiry, like thy sisters before ye who fled moor to moor."

So that's it.

Jews were expelled from England in 1290, and not allowed back until 1656.

The Ladino-speaking Jews from Spain had already fled north, along with the Arab Moors, after Queen Isabella expelled them all. They were called Moorish, for "dark." The Jews who stayed in Spain, the Marranos who hid their faith, kept pork curing in the corner of a front porch to assure passing Inquisitors the home-dwellers were neither Jewish nor Muslim . . . though that pork never entered the house. Some took that custom in fleeing to England.

Hannah had landed in the 1630s, just before slavery was an official trade by law in these colonies, a time when conversion to Christianity could release an African woman from bondage. But what would the Puritans do to a Jewish servant? Where, in any nation, could she hide?

"Enough!" The angry man took Hannah's hands and felt them, probing for calluses and needle-prick scars. "Soft handed and sharp tongued, are ye? A spinster who canst spin? Nor a farmer's daughter useful in a field? What are you worthy for that brought you to this land?"

Then Hannah found her voice. "I am a teacher, *sir,* and not for marrying," she roared. "A scholar for a household, and thankful I can read."

"That is well." A stern, heavy-browed man tapped Hannah on her skull with dirty fingers. "I have now at my Thanksgiving table a Wampanoag squaw who refuses the catechism." He thrust a ten-pound Bible into Hannah's chest. "Come, governess, and give our savage the Word of God."

The pier tilted. The voices of the other women shrank to desperate murmurs. Then, in a blur of transition, it was late afternoon in a low-ceilinged cottage dense with the smell of boiled corn. Under Hannah's thick long skirts, a wooden bench supported her trembling legs. The table before her was heaped with plates of corn and potatoes, deftly set down by a handsome Algonquin serving girl swathed in ill-fitting colonial dress. She looked sideways at Hannah as she bent down with a wooden tray, taking in the measure of her face.

And Hannah almost felt as if she'd been slapped anew, but in a very different way. The immediate recognition was unmistakable, the familiar eye-blink of a moment passing between two lesbians who recognize one another in passing and in that glance wonder, *Will we become lovers?* and regretfully conclude, *No. Can't. But it could have happened. And it would have been terrific.* All of this passed between them in a whisper-narrow instant. But then the young woman slowly raised one finger and ran it over the bridge of her nose.

My face. She's never seen a Jew before but she knows I'm not a Puritan. Not English. I look more like her than I look like them. We both look more like Shoni.

Does she know I see the dyke in her?

"Good," nodded a figure at the head of the table who appeared every inch the family patriarch in all senses of the word. He pointed at Hannah with a half-chewed ear of corn. "Let our governess now go with the squaw to teach our catechism. Remember, these savages are as children, and moreover the men and women seem to mix their places designated by our Creator. We find these women trying to govern and lead, and their men disdaining hard agriculture as womanly, and other deviances. We find the men praising elder women as the wisest of council authorities when we know from our gospel the warning *what man is clean that was of woman born?* So instill in her our scriptures, and both of you remember well the penalty for runaways—for disobedience to both earthly and heavenly Master." He leaned across the table and rapped on Hannah's knuckles, just once, his large and ragged thumbnail scratching her cold skin. Soon enough, Hannah knew, English law would inscribe the "rule of thumb" allowing a husband to beat his wife, or any woman in his household, with a cane or a whip as long as it was no thicker than a man's thumb. By this man's hand, that could mean a stick far rounder than a walking cane. Hannah saw the man's silent wife glance up at her just once, fearful-eyed.

The family's Thanksgiving meal continued, but Hannah and the young servant were directed into a side room filled with barrels, riding boots, and blankets. A leather-bound book lay open to a page on table manners for colonial children:

Never sit down at the table till asked, and after the blessing.
Speak not.
When any speak to thee, stand up.
Look not earnestly at any other.

Hannah had no idea what to do. This, to be sure, was not the lesbian-colony Thanksgiving she and her friends had been dreaming up at Sappho's over warm triangles of pie. This was a test of Puritan decorum, with an added fillip of missionary labor, the erasure of Algonquin women's leadership and stature. She noticed a thinly latched door, beckoning her to flee with her new companion. But that young woman slowly raised a portion of her shirt to show, on one shoulder, the lingering marks of a brutal whipping and, on the other shoulder, a brand. She had twice escaped, only to be caught, returned, and punished with deliberate scarring.

Abruptly Hannah recalled a few words Shoni had taught her in the sweat lodge.

"Wuneekeesuq," she greeted the young woman, who looked startled to be addressed in her own language. *"Wuneekeesuq,"* she responded.

Hannah gestured slowly, first to herself and then to her tough-looking companion. *"Niizh manitoag xkwa. Niizh manitoag xkwa?"* *I am a two-spirit woman. Are you?*

"Niizh manitoag. Naxkohoman," the woman whispered back. *I am a two-spirit who goes between the men's and women's camps, and a singer of songs of my tribe.* She pointed to herself, finally smiling. "I am Weetamoo."

"Hannah. I am Hannah." Hannah pulled out her Jewish necklace, circled her face with her hand, and emphatically pushed aside the Bible she'd been carrying. *"Nkateman." Leave! I had to leave there. That's the only reason women like me are here. But I have to leave here, too. I have to try. Let's go.*

"Nkateman," nodded Weetamoo, but touching her branded flesh. How would they escape without more punishment?

Then Weetamoo pointed to something that certainly did not belong there, in the 1630s, and that Hannah would never have been glad to see in her own time. It was a weapon, poking out from behind a sack of corn flour; but not a Pilgrim musket. It was Officer Angie's gun, the one Isabel did not allow into the bar at Thanksgiving or on any other day, but which their police-woman friend back at Sappho's was obligated to carry close at all times. Weetamoo seized it now and held it out to Hannah. A separate scatter of bullets fell from her hand, rolling around on the wood-planked floor. And Weetamoo sighed, and brushed the clinging flour from her hands as if wiping away an element far dirtier and more sinister.

This was a symbol of all the trouble that would enter this land, plaguing it for centuries: gun violence, first turned against the indigenous peoples, then infecting every community. Forever. Could they stop all of that, somehow? If the two of them— Algonquin and ignorant invader—destroyed this gun, buried its bullets, and bonded with each other, could they reverse the course of history?

Bury the hatchet.

Beat thy swords into plowshares.

Or would Hannah give in to temptation and shoot her way out of servitude, freeing women, slaves, servants, and wives, and some-how fitting all into a different ship that sailed to a female colony?

Then something interesting happened. The bullets melted into kernels. Kernels of corn. The gun grew green, greener, leafy, tasseled—a heavy ear of corn in Hannah's palm. The kernels on the floor rolled into knotholes, disappearing. Then green shoots began to poke upward.

"I don't hear the catechism being recited in there," roared the Puritan patriarch.

Weetamoo leaned forward and brought her lips to Hannah's. The sweetness was indescribable. Their minds locked as well, as the room filled with tall cornstalks. Soon the corn had pushed away any sight of the Puritan hut and they were alone, pressed close in the wild green growth, tasting it on one another's mouths. The Thanksgiving feast.

Yeah. Here's our catechism, you fucker. Remember this.

148

"Hey: Hannah, slow down!" Corncobs, wet and heavy from the serving platter in her arms, were tumbling into the compost cans in the alley behind Sappho's Bar and Grill. But Shoni stood in the doorway, concerned and laughing, wiping Hannah's lip gloss from her cheek. "That was some kiss. What brought that on? White guilt on Thanksgiving? It's okay, you're my *friend*, you goofball. But come back in. There's pie for you."

Mortified, Hannah stood in her own clothes, soaking wet. "I . . ." Had she been kissing Shoni? Where was Weetamoo?

"It's *okay*," Shoni smiled, now, steering Hannah back to the party, the particular lesbian Thanksgiving they had all tried to create. "Leave all that now. Just leave it. *Nkateman*, if you dig. Come on."

They went inside where Isabel had their plates and mugs laid out, where Hannah soon realized, over a final wedge of pie, that Sappho's Bar and Grill was a better-run lesbian colony than she'd ever find in history.

Chapter Eleven
Final Exams

What if it's like a postcard from another part of my life?
Eileen Myles

There was no sound but the scratching of pencils and pens. For the final exam, laptops were forbidden. *Take that, twenty-first century,* Hannah thought smugly from her swivel chair at the lectern. For the last time that semester—indeed, for the whole of that calendar year—and what a year it had been for her own surreal immersion in women's history! Hannah faced the first-year students of her survey course in the basement of university Building B. The lecture hall was actually identified on student schedules as Room B-12, making Hannah think of women's heritage as a sort of power vitamin shot she was jabbing into the firm muscle tissue of young women before it was too late. *Before it's all gone,* she mused, morosely turning the pages of a recent academic newsletter announcing her program's likely name change from Women's Studies to Gender Studies. A student in the fourth row sighed and then sniffled loudly, bringing up other bleary heads and faces. The clock ticked.

Then it was 5:00 p.m. "Time," she called, smiling, forgiving them everything. Her children, her inheritors. And they exploded out of their seats, students she really did love after all. Athletes with ice packs clutched to aching ACL injuries, exchange students, young women she knew were the first in their families to attend college. Scholarship winners, all. And the ones already committed to majoring in women's history, mightily pissing off their parents with this inexplicable choice of study, and the campus feminist activists, half of them in costumes, headed to rehearsal for *The Vagina Monologues*. They surged around her like some hot-wired amoeba, thrusting forward test papers and, in some cases, holiday cards and little gifts. "Merry Christmas, Dr. Stern! Omigod, I mean Happy Hanukah!" They laid chocolates and ceramics on the table, bright folded holiday cards scrawled with gratitude. *You changed my life forever.* This was the high point, the moment that made everything worthwhile. Why would she ever, ever consider a different line of work?

As the last flushed-faced student bounced out of B-12, Hannah listened briefly to their echoing calls: "Did you pick that question on Hypatia? Or did you do Pirate Grace?" Then she turned to the loose pile of 108 final exams. First, before leaving this room, she had to alphabetize that pile, an eye-blurring task she always hated. Dinner afterward: It would wait. And no opening those shiny gift chocolates until Hanukah. But one of her sweet students had actually left her an apple, and Hannah bit into it now, chewing absently while sliding A last names atop Bs, the pile seeming to grow fatter and fatter as she separated names. Rarely did she get through end-of-semester alphabetizing without a paper cut, the dry air thinning her own skin.

Did Miller come before Muller? Of course it did. What was the matter with her? This was exhausting. Narita, Olson, Pensyl— had Pensyl written her final with a pencil or pen? Hilarious. This was taking longer than usual. Why couldn't she focus?

"Ow!" Once again, she'd caught her finger on the splintered podium serving as her lectern in that classroom. "Damn it. *Damn it!*" Hannah put the papers down and peered into her writing hand, now bleeding slightly—well, no real damage done. Not a paper cut but a pricked finger this year. She yanked the splinter out of her hand, feeling tough. Why wouldn't the university get her hugely popular class out of this basement and into a better lecture hall, one with modern, unsplintered furniture? But she knew why. Women's history wasn't a priority. It hardly mattered that she filled the seats, that her students passed, and earned good grades, and after grumbling and begrudging the heavy reading load recommended Hannah's courses to the next crowd of new students. It would always be like this, the oldest and rattiest classroom in the basement of Building B, which everyone joked was haunted, where none of the toilets worked.

Now she was angry again. So tired. Thank God the semester had just ended. Hannah couldn't wait to climb into a hot, hot Vitabath. And take a weeklong nap. Her eyelids fluttered; she was actually close to falling asleep. Well, it was after five-thirty by now; and she really hadn't eaten since eleven, and oh so many papers to grade. She shouldn't go over to Sappho's Bar and Grill until the weekend, though she had promised to meet Isabel for drinks after work in celebration of the last day of classes—and then Hannah yawned. Her head sank down to meet the goddess necklace at her chin. She'd have to grab a cup of coffee before she dared attempt that rush hour traffic drive.

The apple fell from her writing hand, stained with the blood of her pricked finger.

And when Hannah woke, some time later, she was lying on a scratchy bed of hay in some sort of round tower, and at her feet was a broken spinning wheel. She felt quite sure this wasn't Building B.

"Wake up, my sleeping beauty," snarled a voice. "Jesus, Mary, and Joseph. I'll wager you have value, but it sure isn't your hair." The speaker ran a rough palm over Hannah's end-of-semester dyke bob, cackling. "Not enough there to let down for a prince to climb into my tower and save you! Mother of God, what manner gal you be? A passing wench, living as a man? Given up your spinning for the sword, is it?"

Hannah felt the soft lavender fog of enchanted sleep lift from her limbs ever so gradually, tendril by tendril. She was, she realized, chilled and stiff. And hungry. "My apple," she mumbled.

"Apple! Never did a bite of it bode well for woman, not since Eve!" The rough-handed one laughed. "That's what's washed up in my tower tonight: three apple-eaters! And sinners to the core, if you find my meaning!" Hannah saw a face then, freckled, wind-weathered, lively with interest, leaning down to smile at her. "Granuille goes to find your dinner now," the face offered. "There's plenty we took off the Welsh pirateer. I'll be back."

Granuille? There was only one figure in women's history who went by that name: the Pirate Grace of Achill Island, Eire! She was Hannah's favorite extra credit final exam question: *Who was Granuille?* This pirate queen had so fascinated Hannah that one year she visited one of her castles, while vacationing in Ireland, finding a tooth still embedded in the tower wall. Granuille was far more compelling than the ridiculous Peg-Leg Pete characters of pirate comic books from her childhood. Grace O'Malley had plundered, married, remarried, defeated men, acted as chieftain of a clan, supposedly hidden nine tons of accumulated treasure, and was still raiding past the age of seventy in an era when many women didn't live to see forty as housewives.

Hannah remembered now: She had just been administering that final exam when she'd pricked her finger . . . bit into an apple . . . hmmm.

"Hello," came a different voice then.

"Hello, eater of apples," added a deeper voice. "We also love knowledge more than the needle."

"We also paid the price." And the first speaker moved from the shadows, a woman in a toga so marked by scars and burns, flesh so tortured and distorted, that Hannah could only cringe.

"Yes, I am Hypatia," thundered the scarred one. "Torn apart by Christians, hacked to death with seashells, rendered limb from limb and burnt—by monks who didn't want me teaching men. No one will find me beautiful again. And this is Phillis," she gestured with her ridged and unhealed hand, "who was born a slave and grew to be a poet, though no one dared believe her writing was her own." And the great African American writer Phillis Wheatley, another figure from Hannah's fall exam, swished her skirt in curtsey, though directly meeting Hannah's eye.

"We also have some questions," said Hypatia. "We also have a test." And she pulled up a wooden box, stamped with foreign markings of some royal shipping line, and opened up a tiny roll of parchment. Phillis sat down too, her straight back against the castoff spinning wheel. Hypatia cleared her throat.

"To begin. How does a woman in your time live without a man?"

Before Hannah could answer, the door at the top of the tower stairs creaked back open and Granuille stomped in, bearing a tray stacked with boiled potatoes, fish, and brown bread. "How do any of us live?" she snorted. "We steal, or have men steal for us." The taste of the bread was rough and wild and real, the Irish soda bread of centuries, biting back assertively on Hannah's hungry tongue.

She chewed and swallowed slowly, looking at Granuille, at Phillis, at Hypatia—her final exam come to life. And now they were examining her, exchanging glances as their ancient eyes moved across her dark blazer, her Clarks desert boots, her Venus of Willendorf necklace. Had she brought the DNA of her own sweat into this satellite castle, wherever it was? How had Hypatia been brought forward, reconstituted into a breathing scholar again? And Phillis, sent back as well to Pirate Grace's tower? But Grace/Granuille had dared her to explain how an unmarried woman might live in the future.

"I don't have to plunder to survive. Nor do I live on wench's wages," Hannah blundered in the hybrid pirate rhetoric of the hour. "I make my living by teaching about you," she said, hoping to impress her hostess, who, after all, would have been considered a terrorist in Hannah's day. Reaching in her pocket, she found one test exam she'd shoved there to read later, written by her favorite student, Elizabeth.

"Elizabeth! Named for my queen," Pirate Grace gloated.

"We didn't have queens in the colonies; it was meant to be a democracy without monarchs. It ended up a barrier to any women ruling, while those like me were sold. Sold, plundered, and flogged, worse than your piracy," Phillis remonstrated. "I tried to make my living by the pen."

"We had queens and popes, and we could preach and teach men, until they came to kill me," said Hypatia. "They chased me down the streets of Rome. So what is it that keeps us down? I say it is men who limit women's knowledge, who rule them with belief!"

"That's patriarchy," nodded Hannah.

"No," Phillis retorted. "I've had women whip and sell me, and call me by that *word*. We are not linked by sex in women's history. When women jeered me in the slave market where I was sold from Senegal at the tender age of nine years, it was a decent man who took me home and trained me in the classics. I learned Hypatia's subjects, Latin and astronomy. Then as a literate African poet I was received in the very home of a one-time slave-owner, your George Washington. Yes, your founding president and his acolyte Thomas Jefferson, both slave-owners, and my mistress, though a friend, determining my freedoms. So I say it is racial hate that binds us down. That bound me."

"It's racism, as much as or more than sexism," Hannah agreed.

"Arr," said Granuille. "It matters not if fair or femme when food lacks in the larder." She held up a potato as if it were a weapon. "I know my women, centuries hence, will flood the ocean with their starvelings, will cross the ocean belly-flat for work, will sell their bosoms to working men, and find in your land nothing but contempt for their poverty, white skin nary advancing them."

156

"It's classism; it's economic injustice," nodded Hannah. "Oh, boy, the old, old argument in feminism. Which is responsible for woman's suffering. Which do we tackle first? Sexism, racism, classism? Is that what you want to see on my final exam? Yes, it's there. But how about the bias that's uniquely burdened me? Add homophobia." The trio blinked. "Fear of the one who loves a woman as she might a man," she translated clumsily, and they looked at her with wonder and dismay.

"A Sapphic," marveled Hypatia.

"A sodomite," growled Granuille. "Though I have heard it told that women passed as pirates in men's trousers after I had been and gone."

"If women's love blossomed in such ways in Senegal, it's a tradition I was robbed of learning, being brought to Puritan Boston in 1759, where Christianity made room not for loving but for slaves," and Phillis began to recite one of her more famous poems, which Hannah recognized as *Poem on Her Own Slavery*. "No more *America* in mournful strain/Of wrongs, and grievance unredress'd complain . . ."

"I teach that poem," said Hannah.

"Do you have it in my own hand? Not likely," said Phillis, and began writing down the words on a folded paper, which she passed to Hannah's pocket.

"Sex? Color? Class? Love? It can't be ALL!" Hypatia screamed abruptly, walking in circles in the chill round room. "One has to make a choice, to name this battle: What keeps us women down?"

"But there is a word for that—in my time, in my classroom," Hannah tried. "We link all of these problems, and call it *intersectionality*."

Prolonged silence greeted this. Then Granuille snorted, "A word, I'm blessed, that never crossed a priest's lips as he prayed!"

"Or showed up in the writings of an abolitionist," sighed Phillis Wheatley.

"Is it even Latinate?" asked Hypatia. "Why not say crossroads? Better."

"That term has a cross in it," Hannah dared to tease. "On top of everything, I am a Jew."

"A killer of Christ!" gasped Granuille.

"A money-lending usurer," claimed Hypatia.

"And you too bought and sold us, some of you," Phillis reminded.

"Look, I'm none of that. Those words are no better than what you three have been called. Add religious bias to the list! Why don't you take one moment to learn about *me?* I more or less fainted in my own lecture hall just now, dog-tired at end of term from prepping lectures about *you,*" was Hannah's complaint, as if formed from foam and sprayed into their faces. They reeled back and looked at her anew.

Some time later their arguing was interrupted by a bellow floating upward from far below the tower. "No need to ponder your imprisonment further, good kinswomen! Here, I've come to rescue you! Ladies and beauties! Let down your hair!"

Granuille grabbed a pot of boiling water and a quill of arrows. "Prepare to die before you see one hair of any of my wenches!"

"Stop calling me a wench," Phillis remonstrated.

"What can he do to me, that they haven't done already?" hissed Hypatia.

"Who are those guys?" Hannah peered down the jagged walls. "Hey! You there! You're invading women-only space!" she shouted. "And anyway, take a good look. This isn't Rapunzel's tale at all; this tale is feminism. We all have short hair, pal, no length to let down. Buzz off."

They stood, arms locked, the four of them, faces to the window. None of them had hair. "I cannot see when we'll unite again," Hypatia whispered into Hannah's ear. "Does it take invasion to lock arms?" Hannah felt the bones beneath Hypatia's charred flesh; the scars on Phillis's skin. The scrape of ropes and creak of hoisted ladders thudded in the tower's airless space as men below began to climb. All around the tower were men, climbing up to seize them. "They shan't take me alive," Phillis whispered, and Granuille drew her sword.

Hannah came to fully clothed, rumpled and hungry, in her own bed, bits of straw ground into the knees of her good pants. How in the hell had she arrived at home? Had she actually driven her car while in an apple-induced trance? But no, there was a note in Isabel's handwriting on her bedside table: *Got worried when you never showed up after work, so I came by campus and found you asleep in the classroom—drove you home and put you to bed. Car in driveway with keys under the mat. Iz.*

First thing in the morning, she'd take these trousers to her friend Claudia in the chemistry lab and have the straw date-tested to see if it revealed any markers of sixteenth-century Ireland. Then what? No one would believe . . . she fell asleep again, murmuring *sexism, racism, classism, homophobia.* And in the warm room she could hear the whisper of Granuille's voice, sarcastically pronouncing, "Arr, girl, wouldn't ye better count sheep, like us?"

When she really woke again, the straw had vanished from her pants, and the poem by Phillis Wheatley was just a blank napkin from Sappho's Bar and Grill, folded in her blazer.

The next day found Hannah grading papers at home, far from magically empowered lecterns and student-enchanted apples. The only way to get this done was to *do it*, she reminded herself. *When* that day's quota of papers were thoroughly and fairly evaluated, she would allow herself to celebrate with one drink at Sappho's. *Until* then she had to plant her ass in the rocking chair and *grade*. She turned off her cell phone, unplugged the old land-line phone she used to call her mother, made a pot of coffee, and put on what she called "background" women's music: Hildegard of Bingen, Isabel's favorite twelfth-century composer. She stretched and wiggled her feet, clad now in the fuzzy Bugs Bunny slippers an old girlfriend had knitted for her.

The stack of papers beside her seemed to reach to the ceiling, but Hannah felt an odd calm; after all, this ritual of grading final exams occurred every year just before the Christmas and Hanukah holidays. There was no eggnog without grading, no latke without grading. All college professors understood that presents and kisses and mistletoe and menorahs could be enjoyed only after hundreds of grades were turned in to the registrar. If she read twelve, no, fourteen papers a day, for the next eight days, that would do it—108 undergraduate finals, plus those four graduate theses. She would have to be her own Hanukah menorah, burning oil for eight days and eight nights, the miracle being that she finished the job without screaming and was fair, fair, equally attentive and fair to every student who had dared to enroll in a women's history class.

So, where to begin? The finals from her survey course were right there on the scarred wooden coffee table. Each consisted of twenty-five short questions, questions ranging across territory that Hannah herself had mysteriously explored this year (Who was Sappho? Who was Radclyffe Hall? Who is the Venus of Willendorf?) Sighing, she picked up and read through several of these pages in rapid succession, chuckling at replies betraying those who had never opened the textbooks. ("Sappho was a big lesbian. From Lesbos." "Radclyffe Hall was a building in London where they had air raid drills in World War II." "Miriam led the Jews through the Hebrew desserts.") Where's *my* Hebrew dessert? thought Hannah, glancing at the clock. Too early to get up and go burrowing for bagels in the kitchen; read six more.

Part Two of the final exam was far more interesting, if harder to boil down to the flat letter of A, B, or C minus. It was a short essay, inviting each student to respond to the prompt: "If you could go back in time and ask one woman in history any question about her life, who would you choose to meet? What would you ask her? Why?" The students had scribbled furiously, both excited and panicked by the open invitation.

Hannah settled back against the plush cushion in her rocking chair, swirling a carefully measured dollop of cinnamon coffee creamer into her goddess mug. These essays would be a treat. She'd look through whichever grabbed her fancy, to start. No, she should continue to grade alphabetically. No, she should pick out students who were about to graduate and needed their scores first. But what about the international students? They had to have their grades sent overseas early to stern bureaucratic entities who took a dim view of "women's history" on a transcript. Maybe just pick out one favorite student to set the standard. Did she really have a teacher's pet? She would never admit it if she did. Damn it. The clock was ticking. Focus!

The essays were damned good. *If I could go back in time, I would speak to some of the Amazon women from the classical Greek period. How did they instill confidence in other women to become warriors? How were they able to empower other women without perpetuating patriarchy, in a time when women's worth centered around bearing sons for men?*

I'd like to talk to some prostitutes, to "low" women of Babylonian society, and ask what they thought about the ranking of women by reputation that was going on around them. They didn't have the money, literacy, or importance to immortalize their beliefs.

I'd like to know why men decided women were less capable. When did a narrative of difference become a narrative of dominance?

If I could I would choose to ask a Spartan mother if she was satisfied with her level of power. If she is happy simply raising a son up to greatness or if she aspired to be great herself, you know. I personally would rather be a great warrior than a great caregiver of one. I am just learning about history but to me the title of mother of a great man feels inadequate. Being an assistant to greatness, to me, is not the same as actually achieving greatness.

Wow! Hannah could almost feel Hypatia, Phillis and Granuille breathing approval into the wintry living room. She reached for another essay, attracted by its unfamiliar handwriting. And read this.

You see, I have already gone back in time. I am here in your time, now, sitting in your classroom, Dr. Stern, because we use this same exam question of yours in our women's history classes in the future. Are you surprised to learn about your influence, your impact? Well, don't be. As I proposed to my own teacher, I chose to come back and ask YOU my history questions—though sitting in the back row, I've been silent. I waited all term for our conversation.

And now my time is up. On the first night of Hanukah, I'll have to go back. Please, meet me at your club, your Sappho's Bar and Grill, on Saturday night. I hope we may speak there.

Hannah's coffee mug crashed to the floor.

The atmosphere at Sappho's seemed quite ordinary, for once, later that night when Hannah poked her trembling snow boot inside the door and searched for a possible otherworldly guest at the bar. She realized her folly in expecting some Martian space traveler, instead of the time traveler this student proclaimed to be. It wouldn't be a young dyke with antennae or pointy ears, but a futuristic women's studies major. It certainly wouldn't be someone whose presence in her big lecture hall had made her turn and stare. That semester she'd had students with purple hair, pink hair, spiked hair, no hair, modified wheelchairs, tattoos, piercings, henna, sports injuries, and narcolepsy. Everyone had a visible and, more likely, an undetectable "difference."

There was indeed a young woman at the bar she recognized from class, the soccer player, drinking with three other student athletes. So it was Mallory, the goalie! It didn't surprise Hannah that internationally revered *futbol* would still be played, probably with rules unchanged, in some future century. Were female athletes in that future finally being paid equal salaries? Equal bonuses for winning national titles? Could she even inquire?

Then the quiet student from the back row of class (whose soccer games she had neglected to attend even once this fall semester) held up her hand and greeted Hannah. Nodding to the other players, she excused herself: "I have a meeting with Dr. Stern to talk about my paper." Isabel now waved to Hannah as well, directing them to the Nook, where a hot meal had been laid on the table.

They settled in awkwardly. Hannah found herself across from a broad-shouldered twenty-one-year-old (she hoped; Isabel had poured strong drinks for both of them. But wait—what was the legal age of someone from the future, who would not even be born yet in Hannah's own time?). Mallory had a strong Middle Eastern face, Armenian or Palestinian, both pretty and androgynous, with short dark hair in untamed curls and lips swiped by a plum-colored gloss. She wore a very ordinary university goalie sweatshirt, bearing the number 22, cuffs neatly rolled at the wrists. But what in the world kind of wristwatch was that?

"Hi. I'm Mal." The wrist came forward, and Hannah shook her student/time traveler's hand, thinking, *There is no normal way to begin this conversation.* She made an effort: "Do you think your teammates bought that, about your meeting with me here to talk about your grade?"

"They drink here, they've seen you here, they've all apparently seen you *grading at the bar,*" Mal pointed out, and Hannah thought, *Busted. How often had she brought work to finish at Sappho's?* "This is a very ordinary place for lesbians to meet, wouldn't you say? Have I mentioned that I am one?"

Mal spoke with an accent, but it could have been any international exchange student's staccato, lilting English. Hannah looked at her intently. A human being from the future, a young dyke student like the thousands she had taught. Eyebrows, lips, teeth all regular, even refreshingly imperfect. Hannah considered Mal's first words, and decided to begin there. "You called yourself a lesbian; that's wonderful. Is that the—preferred term, still, where you . . . where you come from?"

"No," Mal sipped from her wineglass. "In the twenty-second century we're called tufts. *Tufts,* because we keep our pubic hair, and other women shave. And then we're also seen as tough, so there it is."

"I can get you a Tufts University sweatshirt to take back with you, as a souvenir," was Hannah's next idiotic remark, and Mal laughed. "Already have one, Dr. Stern. We played their soccer team last month and did a team jersey swap. But I wouldn't count on it staying with me. May I ask if you, perhaps, have ever moved through time and brought back what you found there? It would change things in history, right? And we can't have that, right?"

Hannah considered that she had only retained, for all her experiences that year, a Cracker Jack box prize that might have belonged to her ex-lover in 1946, and a fountain pen that might or might not have belonged to Radclyffe Hall. "So, ah—Well, what do you think of our food?" Hannah blurted, remembering how she had reacted to the striking tastes of the fifteenth-century crusts of bread in Granuille's tower, and the sixth century BCE ouzo Sappho had spilled into her mouth so many months (or centuries) ago. Isabel had prepared an oddly high-carb meal for them that night: bowls of mashed potatoes, rice, toast with jam. "Are these your favorite things, from our time?" Hannah asked. "We call this *comfort food.*"

"It's luxurious, fantastic," sighed Mal. "We don't have gluten any more. I've gorged on it for months here. It's such an easy, affordable staple in the dining halls. I'll miss its heft, its mouth-feel."

"The starch has gone out of the future?" Hannah joked, and they laughed. More seriously, she queried: "You must have studied us—the lesbians of this time. My time. If I understand your note, you came into my classroom just to meet me. I'm flattered, of course, as well as terrified. Tell me why. And is any of it what you had expected?"

"The yoga pants are uncomfortable," said Mal. "The material, waistbands, and so on. I prefer the athletic sweatshirts, as you see—the soccer uniform. But I read in one of your books that in your time, there were women's music festivals where everyone danced naked. I wanted to experience that, and I managed to get here the same month that the Michigan festival stopped being held forever. Why did that end? I can't tell you how frustrated

I've been. How did women's spaces end up being seen as oppressive or exclusionary, instead of respected as sacred retreats? Isn't it possible for me to get to another one of those events while I'm here? Can't I have dinner with Maxine Feldman?"

"Well—no," Hannah stammered, thinking: *For fuck's sake, someone in the future reads my books! How about that! And God damn it, there will never be another Michfest.* And, then: *But if she can travel back like this, then any lesbian can get to a Michigan festival—just set the dials for 1979 . . . Will I be able to do that, when I'm eighty? Go back to 1979?* Aloud, she said, "Stop. This isn't real. I'm a historian, so maybe I can communicate with the past. But I can't truly be holding a conversation with a woman from the future! It's not possible!"

"Ah. Tell that to Fiona," smiled Mal, and dug into her mashed potatoes with a long fork.

Fiona. She knew about Fiona! Of course. During her early thirties, Hannah had spent an entire year corresponding with women in "the future." She'd been invited to be a guest speaker at a university in Australia, and preparing for that feminist conference involved weeks of online planning discussions with women's studies colleagues in Sydney. All of their messages arrived in Hannah's e-mail box dated one full day or more into the future. It had felt, then, like a vignette from *Twilight Zone*: Hannah pressed "send" while sitting in America on a Tuesday, and an instant reply came back from Australia dated Wednesday, a kind of voice from Tomorrowland. Then she'd had an affair with one of the conference organizers, Fiona, certainly the most expensive long-distance fling of her life, three or four trips down under, spread across a year. And each time that Hannah flew to Australia she lost an entire day, perhaps departing on Thursday and arriving on Saturday. One of her old travel journals complained, "I had no May 19th this year." But then on the return flight she'd live the same Monday over and over and over again—that is, leaving early on Monday morning from Sydney, flying for twelve to fourteen hours, only to land at the same hour on the same Monday morning in Los

Angeles. On such flights she'd estimate the passage of real time only by feeling the stubble of hair growing back on her shaven legs.

"Then this is just a longer extension of that talkback from tomorrow," Hannah ventured. "But why me? Why did you pick me? If I could go back in time, I'd want to meet ... " and the chill came over her body, as the list formed in her mind's eye. *It's everyone I've met this year. Sappho, Miriam, Radclyffe Hall, Katherine Lee Bates, Liliokalani, Phillis Wheatley.*

Mal had finished eating and was tossing back one after another of Isabel's green-flecked drinks, apparently feeling no ill effect. "I want to tell you this, Dr. Stern. We read your books where I'm in school. You made your mark, yes. We read your *journals*. We know, I know, that you hoped to have been useful, to be remembered. But unlike so many teachers you were able to suspend that boundary between what you taught, what you believed in, and what you experienced as a guide through women's history. You lifted that curtain and showed your students the lesbian past. Even though you live in an era where the recent lesbian past is misunderstood, even vilified, you stood in that historical gap and held that space without apology. To be that 'out' in academia was, we think in my time, fearless." Overwhelmed, Hannah burst into tears, and Isabel hurried over to their table.

"Everything okay here?"

"More than okay," Hannah sobbed. Mal reached for the bar tab with her complex-wristwatched hand, and dozens of five dollar bills spilled from a wallet that opened gracefully as Mal chanted one word: *Pay.*

They sat there for another three hours talking. At last Mal stood up. "Needless to say, I really have to go. But I do have one actual question about our final exam, Dr. Stern."

"I'm pretty sure you'll be getting an A for this," Hannah answered.

"No, it's about the extra credit portion. In the essays, you asked us to pick a woman from the past and ask her questions. Well, that part I've done. But then for extra credit, you directed the class to write a postcard to some woman from the past and *offer her advice*. May I ask how you planned to have your students mail those postcards?"

"Oh—well, they aren't meant for the real mail," Hannah explained. "They drop them in my faculty box. Then I select the best and make a hall display for the women's studies program bulletin board. I don't really direct students to use the U.S. mail."

"But what gave you the idea?" Mal persisted. "We don't have mailboxes any more, you know—and personal handwriting, that's done. I can tell you now, I struggled with writing my tests for you in class! In my women's history class *back home*, we'd use something we call Dynamic Letterbox. But perhaps I've said too much. I know I have. I'm feeling full and sleepy now." And she looked wavy, wavery, close to see-through for the first time, Hannah thought, or was that just the alcohol? Hannah struggled to collect her own thoughts. "Mal, I suppose I first seized on the idea for these writing exercises when I was in San Francisco at the gay and lesbian archives there, and one box in a climate-controlled display for visitors held a letter from Radclyffe Hall. She'd written to some American author, and her return address was clearly on the envelope. I wondered what would happen if I copied down that address and actually mailed something to Hall. She was dead by then, but would a postcard reach her anyway at her old residence? I wrote one and sent it. I remembered that when I visited her tomb this year on my birthday, and . . . I did feel it had reached her, you know. Because . . ." Hannah mused, blushing down into her shirt, wondering what to say about THAT encounter now. And when she raised her head, Mal had vanished, leaving nothing but a dozen grains of rice upon a plate and a college soccer jersey with no body inside it.

167

Only a few of Hannah's students bothered with the extra-credit postcards, and these she found dutifully shoved into her faculty mail box in Women's Studies. But an entire other set of questions and advice for women-who-lived-in-the-past began arriving in Hannah's email on the first day of Hanukah. They came for eight days and nights, glowing on the computer screen no matter what Hannah did with the on/off button, the reboot button, the wall plug, the surge protector plug, the hallway fuse. On one occasion, when a faculty colleague poked her head into the office and chirped, "How's the grading going?," the screen went discreetly dark—and lit up again as soon as the coast was clear.

Nor was it possible to print out and take home the mysterious messages. She tried, but each sheet of paper came out blank, despite fully replenished ink toner in every printer Hannah hooked up to her computer. She gave in to the understanding that these "postcards" were read-only.

Hi! I'm a student of women's history, and my question is: What was it like for you to live as a lesbian in the late twentieth century, when you had no rights?

Greetings, Dr. Stern. I'm taking a class on women's history, and we are assigned to make up a question for a woman who lived long ago as a defender of lesbians. I thought I would ask, what was it like to work at the Michigan festival?

Dear Professor, I wonder what it felt like to stand on the steps of the Supreme Court the day same-sex marriage became legal in America. Did you dance? Did you cry?

Each message identified the writer as a student, about the age of those in Hannah's first-year class, and each had a "mailing" date of December 20th, 2116. Her menorah burned for eight days and eight nights. This year the miracle was not oil, but a different kind of energy. As in Jewish culture, temples might be destroyed, yet the light of culture burned impossibly onward. She

168

could trust this now. And on the last night of Hanukah, when her computer screen faded out forever and no other postcards came, Hannah took the keys from Women's Studies and walked across the snowed-in, empty campus to the locked lecture hall B-12. Going in illegally at night, she wrote in giant letters on the board that favorite quote from Sappho that made her students roll their eyes and sigh.

You may forget but
Let me tell you
This: someone in
Some future time
will think of us.

Chapter Twelve

New Year's Eve

New Year's Eve was the chief moneymaking event and the biggest party of the calendar year for Sappho's Bar and Grill. Usually, Isabel booked some current superstar of the lesbian community as the evening's entertainer and host—an artist everyone really adored at the time, a comedian or blues singer or spoken-word poet (and, one year, a stripper, though unfortunately she had arrived high and fallen off the stage partway into her act.) The flyers for the gala year-end party began to circulate late in November, carrying the promise of yet another opportunity to kiss someone at midnight under the rotating disco ball. Those with homophobic parents and in-laws or other judgmental relatives suffered along through obligatory Christmas and Hanukah gatherings, just waiting to break out their true personalities, and their New Year's outfits and dance moves, at Sappho's on December 31st.

Hannah had slow-danced with Gail at midnight, for many lovely years, and before that there had been several hilarious New Year's dates with other women. Louise, who walked into Sappho's, bumped into the notorious leather-clad biker they all knew as Minnie, and screamed "Oh! No! Not *Margaret!*" before running out the door, never to return. And Chantelle, so uptight about the bar's few remaining smokers (clustered out front in the freezing cold) that she could speak of nothing else, even as Hannah was enthusiastically removing both of their bras in the third stall of the bathroom. New Year's at Sappho's was a night of indecent positions in the corduroy depths of the pit furniture, of aphrodisiac sandwiches shaped like labia, of a dance floor crowded to overflowing with couples in tuxes and glitter and scarves. It was therefore a shock when Hannah, having finally dressed in an outfit that more or less shouted *Hello, I am available,* pulled up to the snow-choked parking lot and saw Isabel's BAR CLOSED sign in the window of Sappho's.

There went her evening! was Hannah's rather selfish first thought. No getting it on with anyone tonight! The possibility of new love—denied! And her outfit so tight she could barely sit down, eat, or breathe. What a waste! Only then did she switch over to practical concern: What had happened? Was there an emergency? Was Isabel all right? She hurried to the door. As her chilled hand hesitated on the knob, the door slowly opened from inside, and there was her old friend obviously in good health, beautifully dressed in purple and green velvet, holding out a golden goblet.

"Good evening," said Isabel, her eyes sparkling in welcome. "For this first hour, I have invited only you."

The bar was decorated with dozens and dozens of heart- and diamond-shaped silver frames, strung together in loops of red cord. They covered the walls, the carved posts holding up the bar, the curtains that billowed around furniture. They were portraits of women from history—both the living and the dead. Some were the women Hannah had encountered during the past year's many unusual incidents. She walked around the warm, familiar room, inspecting each picture: Radclyffe Hall, Granuille, Rose Valland, Sally Hemings. Like baseball trading cards, each image had facts about the woman's life imprinted on the back of the silver frame. These were the women of history Hannah had taught her students to know and to learn from, year after year after academic year. These were the women Isabel had arranged for her to meet, for fresh immersion in what women's history really had been.

She turned to Isabel, who had busied herself at the bar. "Are the other party guests going to see this, or do we take it down in an hour?"

"I have the usual decorations for later," was Isabel's reply. "Don't worry—the big party will go on as usual. Everyone else in the community received an invitation with a later start time than what I told you. I thought you and I would celebrate this year, briefly, together." She pressed the goblet into Hannah's cold hand, and instantly Hannah felt warmth seep up each one of her frosty fingers, up through her wrist, which pulsed. She took one sip, her throat tingling. They sat together in the pit furniture, with their knees touching.

Isabel quoted the poet Ronna Hammer. "Two women touching, just at the knees, but connected/Extending each other like halves of an oyster's shell/The seed of a question/What was the truth protected between them?"

"Well, are you going to take me somewhere else tonight?" Hannah blurted, and a bit of her drink spilled over the side of the goblet and made a penny-sized dark spot on Isabel's knee. "Or just explain to me how you made everything happen this past year? Because I *know* it was you. I don't know *how* it works, or even what it's called, but you sent me places and showed me things. I know some of it starts from these drinks you mix at the bar, which makes me wonder: Is everyone else also getting a trip into feminist history along with their gin?"

"No," laughed Isabel. "You're the only historian here, my friend. Why would I send Letty into the fourteenth century? She just wants to be able to drink gin and breathe at the same time. I make a martini that clears her sinuses." She sighed, as though it were a physical effort to reveal professional secrets. "I do make the drinks women ask for; that's a barmaid's job. But women don't always hear what it is they've asked for. There's a translation only I can hear. It's why any woman comes into Sappho's: for friendship, to feel younger or stronger, to find love, to forget sorrow . . ."

"I've wanted all those things since Gail left me," Hannah interrupted. "But what I usually *ask* for is a vodka and cranberry juice."

"You said, at the top of the year, that you wanted women's history to be your date," Isabel reminded her. "You were holding my special glass when you toasted to that thought. It put me in service to your dream." She moved closer, putting an arm around Hannah. "I didn't frighten you too much, did I? That was never my intention."

"But *how does it work?*" Hannah shouted, and the pent-up consternation made her tightly hooked dress belt pop off; it skittered under the pool table and then lay there curled like a snake. "Yes, I teach women's history—fine. I know how to work in an archive; I could research women's stories myself. How did I become a candidate for *time travel?*"

Isabel, having decided that such an answer required mood music, went over to the sound system and cued up "Sentimental Journey." "Hannah," she said, "one reason it works is because your name is a palindrome. Look at the spelling of *HANNAH*; it's the same back and forth. A person like you can travel back and forth through time."

"*What?* That's ridiculous! Supposing my parents had named me Babs, or Carlene, or *Donna*," Hannah protested, spilling the beans about several girl-next-door baby names her assimilated Jewish mother had considered. "I'd still be the same person I am now, right? I'd have grown up to be a women's history professor anyway, gone to grad school with you anyway. It's just a chance of name. I'd still be worthy of your grand experiment, right?"

"Wrong," said Isabel. "You're Hannah for a reason. The perfect person for the journey. So I waited." She smiled. "I waited for the right year, after I went to graduate school with you, after I had the bar . . ."

The hair on Hannah's arms, head, and belly had begun to

prickle and then stand up. "What are you? Some sort of freaking guardian angel? My feminist history avatar? Casper the dykey ghost? You've just been there all along watching my progress as a women's history detective, and that's why you wouldn't go to bed with me in grad school? Because you had other plans for my life? But wait a minute. God damn it, *you* don't have a palindrome designator name. How come it works for you? This time-tunnel *thing*. Your parents named you Isabel."

"No, not really. I've got another name," said her old friend, and she fixed a look on Hannah that said *MORE GOES ON THAN MEETS THE EYE,* and Hannah had to look away. She sat on the old deep couch, her head bowed between her knees. With the designer belt released from her middle-aged waist, it was possible to bend over and breathe.

Who, after all these years, was Isabel?

Hannah sipped again from the cup Isabel had prepared for her, wondering now what was really in it after all, and she thought of other names that had that quality of palindrome. She thought of how easily she met up with her dead father in dreams, and that she had often called him by the Hebrew word for father, which was *abba*. In English he'd been *dad*. Both were palindromes! But this was women's history, this meeting up with women in the time-traversing spaces of a magical lesbian bar. And Isabel's real name had to be something symbolic of all rebellious women— something short, symbolic of the one who guided knowledge. Which essential, timeless women's names were the same spelled backwards and forwards? Ah, the universal names for mother: Mom. Mum. But no, those were sacred and specific kinds of names.

There were so many popular names for girls in every generation, and quite a few were spelled the same, backwards and forwards. Why had she never noticed this before? In fact, her own aunts were Lil and Viv and Ada. Hannah began alphabetically rummaging through palindrome names that might symbolize women's experience in history, that might hint at Isabel's real name.

Not Tit. Not Pip. Not Anna. But . . . wait a minute . . . why not . . . and her eye fell once more on her black dress belt, curled like a snake under the pool table. It seemed to undulate, just once. A snake had talked to . . .

"Eve?" she ventured.

"Yes, that's it," said Isabel/Eve. "When you move back and forth to all the women of time, remember to start with the first one, or even earlier. In Europe I use a different name, the one for all of us, in French. Can you think of the palindrome in French?"

"Elle," said Hannah. She understood. Universal women. The woman. The first woman. "But why then have you spent years calling yourself Isabel?"

"Time," Iz explained. "I spend a lot of my time helping women of our time understand women who lived in another time. And what's the *sound* of time, in *our* time?"

Bewildered, Hannah thought through her life. All she had ever done—participated in—was school, some aspect of school. She had been a schoolgirl, then a student, a graduate student, a young feminist scholar, a professor—devoted to school, never a year away from a campus ever since age five. Was there a sound to that lifespan? From kindergarten to her work as in women's history, she'd lived by school bells. That first children's TV show, "Ding-Dong School," and later "Saved By The Bell," bells ringing between classes, start of school, end of school, late bell, lunch bell. Then, in college and grad school, alarm clocks. Up. Write. The teaching year, alarm clocks: Up. Teach. Her father, on the day of his retirement, coming home and grandly swinging a hammer at his old bedside radio alarm: Freedom! Time to do as he wished! She understood. There was never enough time, and work time in America went by the clock, and the clock was a bell. Was a bell. Was a bell. *Is* a bell.

"Time is a bell," she repeated. "Is-a-bell. Isabel. *Isabel.*"

As if to bring together illusion and confusion, the clock on the bar suddenly tinged a quarter of twelve, and Hannah saw they had fifteen minutes left in the old year, and what a year it had been, indeed. But—hadn't Hannah arrived at nine p.m.? Just half an hour ago? Wasn't the bar supposed to be filled with other guests by now?

Reading her thoughts, Isabel called to her reassuringly, if enigmatically, "Don't worry, we'll get back to the real party and have an American midnight with our community here. They'll arrive soon, and the clock will go back. We're just cruising ahead a little." Isabel was moving swiftly back behind the bar, where she kept all the rare lesbian books she'd collected from who knew what mystical source or now-defunct women's bookstores of the great beyond. She was opening them up and placing them page-upward on the bar.

"You're going to do Mary Poppins," said Hannah.

"Yes, very good," smiled Isabel, rapidly fluttering every book open. They had both loved and discussed P.L. Travers's lesser-known Mary Poppins stories, including one where all the book characters in the children's nursery came alive in the five minutes before and after midnight on New Year's Eve. The trick was that the magic nanny had opened the books a crack before putting Jane and Michael to bed. Based on their own research in graduate school, Hannah and Isabel had also determined that Travers was a lesbian in her day.

"So are all those characters going to come out of your rare book collection and party with us tonight?" asked Hannah, ready for almost anything now.

"They will if you drink this," Isabel/Eve laughed, handing Hannah a fresh goblet filled to the brim with a sweet brew ringed with tiny flowers. "In a place of radical hospitality, everyone is welcome. All our ghosts, our community's best characters, are welcome here tonight." The ice chips in the glass clinked, releasing musical notes—almost a complete bar of music, in fact.

A bar of music. A bar. Of muse-ic. That was the moment when Hannah finally began to figure everything out. The one individual figure in history Isabel had seemed so interested in during graduate school was Hildegard of Bingen. The botanist and composer. The abbess and the nun. Hildegard devoted her life to classifying healing plants and writing music, both of which she saw as acts of prayer; these aspects were a key portion of Hannah's midterm exam on women mystics of the high Middle Ages. Well, but who had inherited Hildegard's secret plant studies? There were herbs that healed, but also induced visions, hallucinations, and mystical encounters. For Hildegard, the way of a mystic meant hopefully having an encounter with the Blessed Virgin, the Lady, as close to a Goddess figure as the Church had let survive from ancient worship. Others had to have passed along Hildegard's recipes. And for a modern Jewish-atheist-lesbo like Hannah, the equivalent of a mystic trance would be to encounter the great women of the past. It was Isabel who had engineered this.

"I have to ask," said Hannah, looking up and then directly into Isabel's deep gray eyes. "After you disappeared from grad school, you spent a year in Europe. Were you off somewhere, studying herbology with Hildegard? I mean, these plants and potions in the bar drinks. This mixology—it's hers! You were always way ahead of me in reading about her life. I think you found a way to go back, and meet her, and learn medieval magic from her garden. It's certainly what's kept the *bar* alive. The whole community's addicted to these drinks!"

"Do you really need to know?" whispered Isabel, and folded her hands on top of the bar counter as if in prayer, as if in imitation of Hildegard. Then she slowly unfolded left hand from right, and bent her head ever so slightly toward Hannah's in a way Hannah remembered from graduate school days, but with something new, too. There was an opening there. And Hannah thought of openings, doors and time tunnels, and women's spaces opening in the body. With one last sip from the green glass between them, Hannah mustered up the courage to ask the one woman she had always loved, "Are you the portal I keep passing through to find what I can learn?"

"There's only one way to find out," said Isabel, and held out her long-fingered, expert mixing hand.

Hannah took that hand, and took the dare.

The kiss was everything she had ever wanted.

She could never explain why kissing was so sacred to her, the act she had most missed since Gail. Little oral Valentines, waiting to be sent. The fat lively shelf of a pouty lower lip suddenly clamped in her gentlest bite. Then perhaps not so gentle, hungry, oral, oral. Driving fast on a soft curve of road on wheels of lip and tongue. The wandering tongue with its playful capacity to roll like an otter in direct pursuit of pleasure. Like origami, the shape of their mouths opening and folding over and over, *ab initio ad infinitum*. Was she actually thinking in Latin? The comet of lust shooting down from her damp mouth, from lower lip to lowest lip, dew gathering in her vulva. And if all of that in the first kiss, how utterly overpowering to get naked.

But she had tossed off her dress, her dress-up bra, her fragile sea glass necklace, her shoes, her winter tights. Without tights she was indeed quite loose. She felt herself opening up by inches. They fell back into the pit furniture, which had witnessed and supported so much kissing and touching through the years, so much seduction. Isabel's body was not that of a ghost or a chimera. Its warmth was a realism and an answer, unlocking still more doors in Hannah, who bent upward to cup Isabel's face in her own hands.

"Tell me: Do you love women, or do you love only women's history? You have forgotten, haven't you? Or you cannot decide," Isabel teased gently. "You teach the history of the female body, yet neglect your own. Do not neglect mine now." From Isabel's fingertips, leaves and flowers appeared, and vines grew underneath them, making a bed of branches. As the living bed flowered and branched beneath them, Isabel recited from *The Language of Flowers*, never removing her eyes from Hannah's. "Magnificent beauty: Calla Aethiopica. Neglected beauty: Throatwort. Pensive beauty: Laburnum. Bonds of affection: Gillyflower. Consumed by love: Syrian Mallow. Cure for heartache: Swallow-wort. Eloquence: Indian Lagerstroemia. Fire: Fleur-de-Luce. Inspiration: Angelica. Joys to come: Lesser Celandine." She paused. "Love is dangerous: Carolina Rose. Passion: White Dittany. The witching soul of music: Oats. Win me and wear me: Ladyslipper."

The plants in Isabel's hands dissolved into tingling forest tinctures. She rubbed a line across Hannah's left quadricep, which heated and flushed, oily steam curling upward and singing toward the open secret of her yoni. And Hannah begged her, "Open me up slowly; it's been so long."

"Time is just compression," said Isabel, placing the green goblet between her own legs. It whirled with mystery, and Hannah looked into it and saw a wishing well. Coins lay in the bottom, winking brightly.

"Sip it out of me and toast the year," Isabel ordered, her thighs gripping the goblet.

Hannah bent her face down to drink deep and then pulled back, caught in one final instant of hesitation. "No. This can't be happening," she moaned. "I've wanted you for so long, and I *can't*, not now that I know who you are. I can't fuck with *time!*"

"Sure you can," smiled Isabel. "I have." And as the two of them spread open to one another, the books on the bar top also spread, and fluttered. And light streamed from the pages, and the characters came out. And the bar filled up with every lesbian from time.

This was why Isabel had invited no one else, so that this secret list of guests could dine and dance. Now couples rotated about them in costumes long outdated, yet fresh and crisp and perfumed, sharp or sweet. There were cigars and ebony cigarette holders, for no twenty-first century law banning them from bars had ever been enacted. The prewar dykes were freely drinking absinthe, the twenties butches sharing bathtub gin from flasks. The flavors of the lesbian past passed between them as they made love on the old furniture, seemingly on an island in the bar, unnoticed by their foremothers in lust. Hannah tasted drinks in every kiss, old brandy, absinthe, honey mead, ouzo fresh from Lesbos. She was under Sappho, drinking Sappho, seawater in her mouth, alpha, beta, lambda. She was in World War II and Rosie had her riveted to the couch while a band played, Tiny and Ruby swinging jazz with the International Sweethearts of Rhythm. The bold WASPs, Women's Air Service Pilots, buzzed the air, sexy in leather, hair afloat on the winds of time. They tipped up glasses in toast to one another. Drag kings of every era adjusted their ties, reaching with blunted fingernails to stroke the nape of Hannah's neck.

She was making love to the past.

"Not only the past of others," Isabel breathed in her ear, and then Hannah was flying over her own life. Not the span of every woman's history. Her own history. She saw herself at seven, a young Velma in nappy Scooby-Doo pajamas, writing a love letter to her favorite babysitter. She saw herself at nine, crooked teeth large as surfboards as she bit her lower lip in nervous delight, delivering a crushed-out Valentine to the desk of her classmate and idol, Riane. She saw herself reading her first lesbian book, *Rubyfruit Jungle*, eyes wide, the paperback balanced on her knees—one hand shoved deep in a box of Jordan Almonds, and the other hand . . . the other hand . . .

Then Hannah saw the side-street studio apartment where she had first made love with a woman, an older woman, at eighteen. An overcast, blossom-heavy spring afternoon, that room with its open window and pale curtains caught in the breeze. Outside that window the tree branches dropped their sexy, pungent blossoms, leaf and petal, onto the tiny garden patio with its two chairs, a table, a candle melted down in an old Mateus bottle, a pottery bowl full of sea glass. They had left afternoon wine and cheese in that secret patio for the studio with its mattress, the cover already thrown off, sheets eager for their love. Hannah saw this as if sitting in a movie director's chair, a cinematographer's crane, coming forward at low angle.

I am looking into the body of the first woman I really loved.

Her lover then was Sal, age twenty-five, firmly dedicated to the principles of lesbian politics, an athlete. She had long hair, pulled back in a long loose braid with a blue sweatband across her forehead, long legs in old cut-off jeans. She was a *dyke*, they both were then, no reckoning with or room for bullshit, no dresses in their chests of drawers, no bitter on their breath. That passion had been timeless.

She re-entered the scene as it had played out years before, lying on that bed, adoringly under Sal. She entered her own past as easily as a hand into warm water.

Hair flowing over arm, lips on the beating vein of her own soft neck, the pillow scattered below her. Sal was on one knee, her tongue inside Hannah's navel. Hannah knew again the images and sounds that stayed with her to this day: five drops in a wine-glass, the distant crunch of car wheels passing somewhere, birdsong trilling, sheets of paper flapping on an end table, empty pizza boxes, wooden floorboards creaking with a snap as Sal stood up and pulled her thin tank top over her head. Hannah said again the words she'd stammered on that afternoon: *Hold me. Tell me something. Tell me what to do.*

Her fingernails softly touching Sal's breasts, breasts that never lived in bras. She was groaning with the beauty of Sal's profile. And the gray day bloomed in violet and rose.

Rose. She rose. She rose upward and over to that open window and the hours had passed to nighttime, coming in with urgency and voices.

"Moonlight," Isabel called out. And then she was with Isabel again, and they were standing up in dark woods more modern than Sappho's time. It was not wartime either. This was still Hannah's early past, and it had to be a women's music festival because Hannah could hear guitars and owls and kitchen-refrigerator generators turning on and off. Isabel reached out to her face. It was Hannah's first festival kiss all over again, she was nineteen again, the first tentative flesh of mouths so gently open, electric heat in seconds. Branches snapped underfoot as they shifted in clinch, their hips adjusting, pelvis-to-pelvis. The sweet green scent of a crushed fern filled Hannah's nose. Then her nose was sideways under Isabel's nose and her top lip in Isabel's teeth. Then Isabel's teeth were biting off Hannah's buttons. Yes, that was how it had happened, so long ago in her own life.

There was drumming in the distance; it intensified. "Go ahead, now," Hannah heard herself groan. But Isabel paused and in a low voice commanded, "No, not yet. Not ahead. Back, earlier," and the earth underfoot became soggy, mossy, the moonlight interrupted by tall figures. Women were meeting at a water source nearby. One figure, clad in mail, came toward them.

"Vous?" whispered somebody young and strong, and then "Elle?," and Isabel was Joan of Arc. Her short hair brushed against Hannah's exposed breasts. She raised her face and laughed "Ne, je ne regrette rien." Her warrior hands dripped spring water onto Hannah's nipples. Hannah threw out her arm and her open hand found a stump. It throbbed like a heartbeat under her damp palm. It was alive.

"I will fight," said Joan. "Do not fight *me*." And Hannah gave in, gave in, did not fight. Her hand flat on the beating stump, spring water beading on her backward arching neck. "Into battle now," Joan breathed, peeling off chainmail. "I will command you. Ride."

She felt walls at her back. Ancient walls, walls of every texture across time, walls other lovers, other women had leaned against. The jagged roughness of a limestone cave, the smoother but cold masonry of castles and fortresses. Locked towers, watch towers, rooms with rusted locks and latticed windows. Corrugated iron walls, blazing hot in summer, palm-thatched walls, scratching her with tropical scented heat. Flocked wallpaper, gilded upholstered walls, curtains, all at her back as Isabel pushed, leaned, locked thighs with her across time in a geography of desire. A timeline of desire.

She had been up against a wall for so long, her mind open to the past, yet keeping her back to her own present, to the possibilities in her own lifetime. Her own *now*. She had always liked making love standing, but finally at year's end this wall at her back was no longer the dead end of a finished relationship she could not return to and redecorate, fix up. She was making love standing because she was eye to eye with all that, level, anchored. Anchored in herself. Anchored in permission to explore desire again.

Her body relaxed. She let herself move forward and lean in. She felt her writing hand rise up like a door latch giving way to openings, to access, and her hand touched strands of hair on Isabel's long neck. It was Isabel, again, Isabel after all. They swayed. The back walls vanished. The light around them was a perfect circle, the motion particular to just one function: a disco ball. They were on their way through history back to a lesbian bar. It was the 1970s.

She saw Trale, Trale at a younger age, Hannah's own age, holding another woman close with dapper-clothed arms. She heard a familiar sneeze and saw Letty, her gray hair now sharp black, as sharp as her suit coat and tie, cracking a pool ball and laughing, big as life in the center of a trio of admirers. But the musicians onstage were women no longer alive in Hannah's present-day time. They were the musicians of the early women's music movement, Kay Gardner, Maxine Feldman, Gwen Avery, Therese Edell, Janet Small, Ginni Clemmens. Pat Parker was reading poetry at the mic. The air reeked of patchouli and marijuana and unshaven armpits and sex.

Pushed forward by some unnameable urge, Hannah moved toward Trale and said, "May I cut in?" ignoring the glare from Trale's elegant partner. She placed one hand around the older woman's waist. Except Hannah was the older woman now, or perhaps their ages were exactly even just for this one moment, and there was no "firmly" in Hannah's gesture. Objects and limbs had a wavery quality. She had the feeling that her body had passed right through Trale's date. But they had both seen her, had shifted to accommodate her, and Trale was smiling, saying "Hmm. Have we met? I don't think I've seen you here yet."

"I'm from . . ." Hannah began, thinking, *the future of the bar*, and settling on "California." It sounded ridiculous. Then she realized Trale had said, "I haven't seen you here *yet*," not the standard "I haven't seen you here *before*." She had forgotten that Trale was able to see figures past and present. She was recognizing Hannah from the future.

"You're thinking too much," Trale interrupted. "This is a trip you should be enjoying. It's okay; I think we've been friends before, probably in an earlier life. Plus, it's New Year's Eve." She led easily, moving Hannah around and around the floor as the band played set after set of classic 1970s women's music. Overhead, the disco ball swayed, sparkling from that same square of air in which it swayed in Hannah's own time. A square of air overlooking love and community for four or five decades. This was where the time capsule was hidden, she suddenly remembered: hidden in the disco ball for someone long after the '70s, '80s, '90s, or Hannah's own bar years to discover anew. History, lesbian history, twirled and sparkled overhead. But, obeying Trale, she stopped thinking. Her body relaxed. Sisterhood felt good. She was linked to the past through Trale's broad shoulder, and now they were the same age, the same era, the same feeling in their hearts. The movement would go on forever, Amazon women rising, and they would never age. Creators and inheritors of women's culture were one and the same. And the bar would always be there, with both of them care-takers of its time capsule.

Slowly, they danced together. They turned together. And time turned around them. Then Trale said, "Okay, Doc. Catch you later down the road," and she went back to her real date for that par-ticular New Year's Eve—leaving Hannah wondering how, if they had yet to meet in some time-distant lesbian future, Trale could know *in 1974* to address her as *Doc*. For certainly, during their fleeting mystery dance, Hannah had not told Trale her name.

Then, hours or years later, it was once again Isabel against Han-nah's neck, and the bar was empty of 1970s revelers. Isabel whispered, "We're heading back now. Flying fast on that secret airplane, my darling, and when we land, I promise you everything will be as we left it, with one full hour before everyone else comes into the bar for the regular New Year's Eve party." When Hannah opened her eyes again, they were back in the pit furniture, Isabel's legs still entwined crisscross with Hannah's. The double X. The bar was lined with delicious dishes of food from every culture and city, all of it palindrome-named food: Indian *na'an*, Hawaiian *ono*, Lebanese *shish 'bab*, American soda *pop*.

Hannah reached up and touched the soft point at the end of Isabel's Gallic nose, tracing the slightly bumpy runway up to the open space between her eyes. Those eyes crinkled and closed with pleasure. Once more Hannah murmured, "Are you real?"

"I'm real wherever I am, blood, tissue, menstrual issue, everything," Isabel avowed. "It's just that I'm able to *move around*. And now you can, too." She reached under the couch and picked up a painted toy airplane, a glider probably hidden and forgotten by Susie or another child during last week's family Christmas party.

"I can move around, too? You mean—there's more to come?"

"There may very well be," and Isabel moved the toy airplane through the air, humming, moving it, Hannah understood, through time. This was Isabel's way of saying that they would move through time together. Did that mean partnership—or visits with other women of the past? She didn't care. It was all good. Bring it on. She parted Isabel's thighs with her own, whispering, "I'll choose the place this time. Take me *there* again."

Chapter Thirteen
Thirteen O'Clock

Much later still, when the tumble of time finally released them in a tangle of damp hair and honey mead dribbled on their skins, Hannah raised her head to find she was sprawled right on top of the bar, and the digital clock by the cash register was, impossibly, blinking thirteen. Isabel removed her lips from Hannah's long enough to say "Happy New Year."

"Not yet," Hannah replied.

Isabel brushed Hannah's hair back over each ear. "I've waited twenty years to say these words to you—but if I do, they will change everything, and you will have to trust me and believe what I am saying. And we'll journey from there." Hannah's legs were trembling for the words she hoped to hear. Would it be a declaration of love? *Now she will say "I love you,"* Hannah willed, her entire body drawn toward that phrase, those three words, that new beginning. She tried to keep her eyes on something ordinary: the brown, scuffed floor of Sappho's Bar and Grill. For some reason the little toy airplane had vanished.

Isabel followed her gaze, and what she said was fully unexpected. "Yes, I know, the plane has disappeared. But, listen, Hannah," she breathed urgently. "It's fine. That's the place we have to go next, in the New Year. Things are going to change. Because *I know where Amelia is.*"

A peek into

Sappho's Overhead Projector
Chapter One

Hannah left the meeting in the dean's eighth-floor suite determined not to cry. No, she wouldn't give him the satisfaction. Her
face stonily composed, she walked to her office and began to
yank pushpins out of the walls, sending her framed art posters
crashing onto the worn industrial carpet.

No tenure for Dr. Stern. Her position was going to be *termi-
nated.*

The entire history program had apparently been targeted for
"strategic downsizing." Just two tenured professors—both
male—would remain, folded into a hallway behind the study-
abroad unit. Women's history would be eliminated as a major. "It
has been a bold experiment here," the dean purred. And Hannah's former office? Her beloved townhouse building was going
to be turned into a new subway stop.

Goodbye and good luck. Hope you find work somewhere else,
sister.

At 6:00 p.m., worn out from a lonely day of packing up her office,
Hannah sank back into the bathtub, adding Lux until a foam of
argan-scented bubbles covered her breasts. But no fragrant oil
could soothe her skin; no alcohol in the house came close to
numbing her panic. She'd have to go over to Sappho's Bar and
Grill later on, let Isabel make her a potion. Food, though, seemed

to whet her appetite for rage and revenge. Chipotle chocolates in particular. She nibbled one now, smashing another with wet fingers and smearing it into a bronze-hued women's symbol on the tile wall. Then she shut her eyes and visualized, again, the line of urban Metro representatives who had swarmed so importantly through her office the other day. Plucking blueprints from crisp folios, they had measured her office shelves and walls for imminent destruction even as she sat there tapping final grades into her computer with all the concentration she could summon. Erasure. Erasure of her time there, twenty years of grading in that space.

The next day, as Hannah grimly piled her art and syllabi into old watermelon crates and boxed up textbooks she'd taught for years, she worried that she might leave something valuable behind by accident. Could a class outline get stuck on a nail, in a crack in the wall, or slide under the old tacked rug? And if so, when the snug egg of her old existence cracked under phallic drill bits of subway renovation, would the underground workers far below find evidence of her teaching life, trickling down like cave moisture? Jutting out of the underground walls like jagged gems of feminism in a diamond mine? Would fragments of her old class notes be discovered years or centuries later, lost bits and pieces preserved and entombed like those amber-trapped insect bodies in the Jurassic Park movie, holding within the DNA of women's studies as it was once taught? Would her lesson plans be *discovered* one day like the Dead Sea Scrolls, like Sappho's poetry, like cave art on a Neolithic wall, as the Venus of Willendorf statue herself had been found? Only this time it would be not archaeologists, but Metrorail workmen in scratched hardhats, marching through a dirty tunnel space with pickaxes under their arms like the Seven Dwarves?

And then the light bulb came on full beam above her head. *What if all that Neolithic art, those goddess statues, the evidence of women's sacred feminine past that male explorers found in caves, was just the left-behind teaching material of an even more ancient women's studies professor? Someone whose office . . . UP THERE . . . was shut down and destroyed? Like mine?*

Supposing the art slides Hannah used in her class lectures on women's heritage were merely proof of goddess figurine toys that had accidentally slipped off the desk of some earlier, earliest grand lecturer, as uprooted and bereft as Hannah felt now, but uprooted from where? From *UP THERE?*

All right. Who was the giant professor up above, the lesson planner in the heavens, the great overhead women's history department chair who had lost her place and floated in space? How could Hannah—and maybe Isabel, too—find her, restore that lost department in the sky, and even join it as a lecturer again?

Would she have to be . . . dead?

On Tuesday, having surrendered her university ID and office keys, Hannah walked disconsolately into Lecture Hall B-12 for a final nostalgic visit. Here, she had made the past visible, selecting what she believed students must know about women's differing histories. She gave a loving pat to the wobbly overhead projector, now shoved into a corner, its long electric cord wrapped like a protective dragon's tail around an aging body. This had been her old standby when DVD films failed to load; just images laid over a light box, projected against the two big screens. Sappho, Queen Liliokalani, Bessie Jackson. How it made them real, huge, larger than life, undeniable!

She was alone. She was on her way to nowhere, fired at middle age. This lecture hall had been her kingdom, or queendom, or playing field. Dr. Hannah Stern is in the house; start note-taking! Well, who would come in and stop her if she taught one last lecture now?

In her pocket was a brochure for the Mediterranean goddess

cruise she'd planned to take … before losing her job and needing a whole new budget. No Olivia cruise this summer. No fun ever again. Well, she could dream for free. She slid the brochure onto the surface of the projector. She'd project images of happy lesbians, partying on a ship's deck, as her last stand. Her *Bon Voyage*.

And both of the dual wall screens lit up. The projection whirred to life. Sappho's face rose, rose up on the huge light panels, watchful, fierce, benevolent. Hannah jumped back, stupefied. *But I didn't plug anything in yet. In fact, I couldn't have turned it on. My passcode was just cancelled. I no longer have my university ID!*

Then the lecture hall filled up with every student she had ever taught, two or three to a seat, holding in their laps spiral notebooks, sketchpads, computers, day planners. Every pen and finger was raised up to start note taking.

"Walk right in," boomed Sappho's voice, undulating from the overhead projector. "And sit tight now. All of you. Listen to me, sisters. We're going for a ride."

About the Author

Bonnie J. Morris is a women's studies professor with twenty-two years on the faculty of both Georgetown and George Washington University; accruing multiple teaching awards from both institutions. She is the author of 15 books, including three Lambda Literary Finalists (Eden Built By Eves, Girl Reel, Revenge of the Women's Studies Professor), two national first-prize chapbooks (The Schoolgirl's Atlas, Sixes and Sevens) and the critical feminist texts Women's History for Beginners and The Disappearing L. Her recent exhibit on women's music at the Library of Congress broke new ground in showcasing lesbian albums, and she is now a historical consultant to the Smithsonian Institute, the AP U.S. History exam, Disney Animation, the State Department's International Visitor program and the Global Women's Institute. She may be found lecturing on C-Span, Olivia Cruises, Semester at Sea, the National Women's Music Festival, and on Pacifica Radio KPFK.

Acknowledgments

This unusual book drew support from many friends and colleagues who offered suggestions, getaway time, and nourishing love. I am particularly grateful for the gift of writing time at Hedgebrook; Women's Week in Provincetown; the hospitality of friends in Kauai; and the warm home spaces of Lillian Faderman and her partner Phyllis. Enthusiastic feedback came from Jennifer Wisdom, Jeanette Buck, Alison Bechdel, Woody, Liz and Jane. For the original experience of belonging to Herizon in Binghamton, New York, there are not enough words to express loyalty and affection. Thanks as well to Liz McMullen and Doreen Perrine for daring to publish the first small excerpts from these tales in their anthologies *Appetites* and *Haunting Muses*. Finally, I am delighted to be a Bywater author, and for the warm support of editors and associates Salem West, Kelly Smith, Elizabeth Andersen, and the extended family of the Golden Crown Literary Society.

Bywater BOOKS

At Bywater Books we love good books about lesbians just like you do, and we're committed to bringing the best of contemporary lesbian writing to our avid readers. Our editorial team is dedicated to finding and developing outstanding writers who create books you won't want to put down.

We sponsor the Bywater Prize for Fiction to help with this quest. Each prizewinner receives $1,000 and publication of their novel. We have already discovered amazing writers like Jill Malone, Sally Bellerose, and Hilary Sloin through the Bywater Prize. Which exciting new writer will we find next?

For more information about Bywater Books and the annual Bywater Prize for Fiction, please visit our website.

www.bywaterbooks.com